LOLA

LOLA

A Hero's Journey

A Gift for a Lifetime IV
by WILLIAM FREEMAN

1

LOLA

Represented by:

FREEMAN LAW P.A.
LEANNA S.A. FREEMAN
255 West King Street
St. Augustine, Florida 32084
legal@freemanlawllc.com

Booksonnet.com

LOLA

For
LANA

LOLA

Cover art by STARR EMERSON

LOLA

PART ONE

Lola was on a cruise ship deck, standing next to the rail, playing cellphone games with Victor. They were about the same age. The cruise was a present from her family for her sixteenth birthday. She wore floral printed tights, flip-flops, and a sports bra covered by an oversized blue men's long-sleeved shirt. Her brown hair was shoulder length. Victor wore his crew uniform, black pants, and a white short-sleeved shirt with epaulets on his shoulders. He had a radio on his hip that connected him to the rest of the crew. It was nighttime.

"I'm going to be a lawyer," Victor said.
He moved close to Lola and showed her a picture on his phone. He was wearing a black robe holding a thick book in white hands. His hair and eyebrows were thick and black. His face was dark brown with big brown eyes. He wore a broad smile that showed straight, white teeth.
"What's wrong with your hands?" Lola asked.

LOLA

"I photoshopped my face onto Ruth Bader Ginsberg." He laughed. "Here, look at this one."

"What happened to your hair?" Lola said.

"Albert Einstein," he said.

"You have great aspirations," Lola said.

"Who are you, and what do you want to be?" he asked.

"I haven't decided," Lola said.

"I can do anything I want," he said.

"I feel the same way," Lola said. "Once I make up my mind."

"Text me a message," Victor said. "That way, I'll have you in my contacts."

He held her hand with the phone. He typed in his email address. They were shoulder to shoulder and face to face. She moved away but did not stop looking into those dark eyes.

YOU ARE A VERY HANDSOME MAN, she wrote.

He looked at his phone, smiled, and wrote back: YOU ARE A VERY BEAUTIFUL WOMAN

Lola read the message. She looked at Victor, and they both laughed. They both had the same sense of humor.

"Let me show you something special," he said. "Follow me."

The cruise ship was large. Four trips around the main deck equaled a mile. It was many stories high with endless inner cabins and outer cabins with balconies. Inside were three restaurants, a cafeteria, and a lounge with an endless supply of food and drinks. There was also a swimming pool and game room. There was a ballroom with a band. Those were only the places Lola had seen.

Victor led her through a coded door by the pool. He punched the code into a lock, and they passed through, closing the door behind them. A landing was well lit, and they descended a metal staircase to a lower passageway that ran between an inner hull and an outer hull. They passed other coded doors on the inner hull and other crew members going in and out. The crew members all nodded to Victor and smiled with knowing eyes as they went about their duties.

While they walked, they talked.

"My country has a middle class," Victor said, "but all you ever see are refugees, violence, and disasters."

"We have poor people too," Lola said. "But if it bleeds, it leads in the news. I think it's the same all over the world. We are all the same."

"But in my country," Victor said. "We don't shoot our children in school."

There was more to him than just a pretty face.

The corridor became narrower, and the engines' sound became louder and then quieter as they reached the end. To the right was a large watertight door sealed shut. To the left was a smaller door. Victor turned a wheel in the center of the door that unsealed it and opened it to the outside and the sea.

The door swung open to a metal platform enclosed by a metal railing. It was more than large enough for two people. A metal ladder extended from the platform up the outer side of the hull to the main deck some distance above them.

"What is this place?" Lola asked.

"It's an escape hatch for the engine room," Victor said. "That large door behind us goes to the engines. Some of the crew bring their girlfriends outside here for some private time."

LOLA

Lola eased herself away, but she was still close enough to Victor to smell his cologne. It was Old Spice. She smiled and looked at him.

Looking back at the door, Victor said, "There is a sensor that signals the bridge when the door is open, but it happens so often that by the time anyone arrives to inspect, the door is closed enough to stop the signal."

"So if we close the door, no one will know we are here," Lola said. "And no one will come to check on it."

"It can only be opened from the inside," Victor said, "to protect against pirates."

"Pirates!" Lola laughed. Victor laughed too.

"Let's go outside." Victor took her arm by the elbow to help her over the lower frame.

"It's very special," he said, closing the door behind them enough to stop the signal.

The floor of the platform was a metal grid. The safety rail and ladder were also metal. All painted white with occasional rust spots. Below them was the sea. Above them, the hull of the ship rose like a cliff.

The rush of the sea was constant, as was the wind while the ship moved forward. The rhythm of the engines vibrated through the steel. It was cool and wet to the touch. The ambient light of the ship reflected off the black sea. It was a moonless black sky decorated with a canopy of a billion stars.

Lola moved to a corner of the rail that came above her waist. Victor moved close to her to hear his voice as he showed her his cellphone. He pressed against her. She flinched. He put his arm around her to keep her safe.

"If you lay down and look up, you can get lost in the stars," he said.

LOLA

They were face to face with his arms around her. He pulled her close. He kissed her.

The radio on Victor's hip began to vibrate. She moved out of his embrace. He had to answer it. His smile turned to a frown.

"I have to go," he said. "It's my job."

"Saved by the bell." Lola let out a sigh of relief.

"I'm sorry if I am too bold," Victor said. "I'll be back in a few minutes. You are not scared to wait, are you?"

"No," Lola said. "I can find my way back alone. But I would like to stay and look at the stars."

"I will hurry back," he said and was gone through the door.

Lola took a deep breath and lowered herself to the grated floor. It felt like a bed of nails, so she laid out flat to ease the discomfort. It wasn't so bad with the sea below and the stars above.

There was too much light coming from inside where Victor had left the door open until someone came by and closed the door without seeing her.

"Damn deck crew," she heard a man say as he turned the wheel to seal the hatch.

"What have I got myself into this time?" Lola said. She could hear her parents criticizing her "self-confidence and overly adventurous spirit."

"I hope Victor comes back soon."

She had wanted him to kiss her. She had pulled away. She was not that kind of girl.

Lola did some breathing exercises, and tension drained from her body. She was not afraid of Victor. She had a second sense that warned her about dangerous people. She needed it with her "overly adventurous spirit" that sometimes brought her to the edge where the universe kept her from falling off.

It had brought her to rest on a small platform above the sea on the side of a very large ship with the wind picking up. It was getting cooler, and all she had to warm her was the shirt her big brother had given her so she would be dressed properly for her birthday dinner. It was a wonderful party full of stories and laughter. She loved them all so much it brought a smile to her lips and a tear to her eye.

Her parents had gone to the ballroom to dance. Her brother had gone to the ship's library to read a book. She had gone back to the room they shared to journal when Victor came in to bring an extra blanket.

Lola had been writing on her phone.

"Is that a ten?" Victor asked.

"Yes," Lola said and looked into those enchanting brown eyes.

"I have one too," he said, moving over to where she was sitting. "We are soulmates."

"Virtually," Lola said, and they both laughed. He had a nice laugh but turned quickly and was gone. There had been a connection.

Later, when she was strolling around the deck, she saw him again. He challenged her to a video game. She was up for it. That's how it all started.

The universe had brought her to the platform where she could look out between the bars that supported the rail. It was like a small prison cell. The sea was dark. The wind was chill. Lola began to shiver. She looked up at the ladder that led to the deck. She looked at the blackness of the sea and the star-filled sky. The ladder looked like a stairway to heaven.

LOLA

Lola stood up.
Who was she? What did she want? Life, love, and warmth.
Climb that ladder.

She took her phone out of her shirt's breast pocket. She could call Victor for help. She scrolled down her contacts and selected Victor. She was directed to a voice mailbox. She tried to speak calmly, but the shivers, the sea, and the engine's sound garbled the call. At least he would know that she called.

She put her phone back in the breast pocket of her shirt and faced the ladder. She kicked off her flip-flops. The wind blew them against the bars of the rail at the end of the platform. Automatically she bent down to save them from being blown away.

In its waterproof case, her phone bounced once, then found its way between the rails and escaped into the sea.

Her choices became limited. Wait in her cold cell or climb that ladder. She made a decision.

She was an athlete. She was a dancer. She was a swimmer. She did gymnastics. She was a runner. She had climbed mountains and walked canyon trails. Her legs were strong. Her arms were strong. She was confident. She could do this.

Lola faced the ladder and grabbed the highest rungs she could reach, and pulled herself up until her feet engaged the lowest steps. The metal was grooved for traction, not smooth. It dug into her hands and stung. Her feet rebelled at the cut of the metal.

Lola paused to breathe deeply to settle herself. She eased into the pain and became steady. She started to climb.

She stopped halfway up. It wasn't that difficult. She was calm. The shirt fluttered in the wind. It was a nuisance. She stood on one foot and held on with one hand while trying to unbutton it from the bottom to take it off.

LOLA

As she reached the buttons at the neck, a gust of wind blew up her back billowed the shirt out. It became a parachute that lifted her foot off the step and away from the ladder. Her one hand on the upper rung was the only thing that kept her from being blown away. Then the parachute collapsed, and she lost her grip.

She fell.

Her first thought was hitting the platform or the rail. She saw the rail as she passed it, reaching out with the thought of grabbing it, but the fall was faster than the thought, and she prepared to crash into the sea.

She wasn't sure how far it was to the water. All those hours at the pool were on her mind, the jumps and dives from the ten-meter platform. She took one last deep breath. She pulled in her arms, put her feet together, looked straight ahead, and closed her eyes. She pointed her toes to decrease the impact. She entered the water smoothly. She stuck the landing.

The shirt spread out as a drogue ending her descent, and she kicked her way to the surface, where she saw the cruise ship moving past her.

The propellers that drove the ship created a vortex that pulled her back into a whirlpool of certain death. With all her might, she swam down and away from danger until the vortex caught her, spun her around, and spit her out onto the surface, where she grabbed the first breath available just as the wave from the ship's wake slapped her in the face. She spit out the mouthful of seawater, blew her nose, and turned onto her back.

Lola couldn't remember a time when she couldn't swim. From rolling onto her back as a baby in her grandmother's sixty-foot lap pool to swimming underwater from one end of the pool to the other, racing against her grandmother with a strong kick and finally winning. Lola was at home in the water.

Kicking to stay afloat, she unbuttoned the shirt's sleeves to release her arms and pulled the back around in front of her. She put her arms back into the sleeves and raised the shirttail high in front of her until it caught the wind and formed a bubble that she pulled down to her waist and tied around her back. She rested in her flotation device. It would hold the air as long as it remained wet. It was something her grandfather had taught her from his days in the Air Force. It worked. It really worked.

Lola turned to see the ship moving away. Its light faded until she was surrounded by darkness except the infinite stars filling the moonless sky. She was alone in the sea. Lola breathed slowly in measured breaths as she assessed her situation.

She was alive.

From the ship, she had seen a few scattered lights on a distant shore, but she didn't know how far it was. A ghost ship without lights passed in front of the land lights. The current seemed to be pulling her further into the black night. The bubble still held but was getting smaller. She looked up at the infinite universe. Lola's grandfather had told that in an infinite universe, there were infinite possibilities. If one of those possibilities was God, none of the others mattered. She prayed.

Victor had gone back to the platform and found the door sealed. He opened it and saw no one. He supposed that Lola had gone back to her room, upset that he had taken so long to return. He had her number, so he texted her.

LOLA

Lola looked at the universe from her spot on the sea. She was just an insignificant speck. She was miles from land. She would have to swim as long as it would take.

"I'm a hero," Lola said to the universe. "I can do this."

A wave of doubt came over her with a wave that broke over her bubble. She cleared her mouth and nose and floated on her back. She was suddenly tired. Her self-confidence and adventurous spirit were not enough. She looked up at that endless universe that possibly held a God.
"I give myself up to you," Lola said.

Alone.

There was a vibration in the water behind her. There were bells and a light in the water. She swam to it. It was her cellphone.
There was a famous picture of Mohamed Ali standing victorious over a fallen opponent. He had Victor's face.
Lola laughed, and hope welled up in her.
There was a pop-up.

LOW BATTERY.

Her smile turned into a grimace. Should she try to return his call? Should she call her mother? Would she have enough juice to explain her situation?
"Who am I?" Lola said. "I'm alive. What do I want? I want to live."

Mistakes were made, but that was history. Her future was undetermined. She loved her family and wanted to see them again.

LOLA

She loved the sea as an extension of her life, not her death. What could she ask for? Be careful. It might come true.

There was a story in the Bible.

A king in battle told God that if He granted him victory, he would give up to Him the first thing that he saw, his greatest treasure. His crown. His throne. The king rode victoriously into his castle. The first thing he saw was his precious daughter.

It was not wise to make deals. Heaven had no quid pro quo. This for that. There was only this life. Be thankful for that.

How many minutes did the phone have left? Would it even work bouncing in the waves? Her eyes had adjusted to the starlight and phosphorescence in the water that showed motion. She felt something rough brush against her bare foot. She turned on the light on her phone. For the first time, she was terrified.

A shark!

She was eye to eye with a shark that was longer than she was. She looked into that eye, a black hole that led directly to hell. Was this how life ended?

Lola had been doing the sidestroke to conserve energy, holding her phone out of the water so she could make a call. Her heart pounded so loud it wiped out the sound of the sea and the wind. Her mind was racing.

Racing! The butterfly stroke. She never thought that she would use it in real life. Now it was her best option. She turned on her stomach. She brought her hands forward and then down, then up out of the water, reaching forward and down hard. Her cellphone was in her right hand, and when her arms came down, she struck the shark on its nose. The shark dove down and away, leaving a trail of glowing green phosphorus.

15

LOLA

Lola took a calming series of breaths. She turned on her phone light again and shined it in the direction the shark had fled. From the glow of the sea, she could see that it had turned.

Lola loved her life. She loved her family. She loved the sea and the sky and all the earth. She even loved the shark that was coming to take her life. The shark.

No!

Sharks!

There were three of them.

Three dorsal fins coming toward her. The big one that had turned and two more from the side. As the big shark rolled to attack her from below, the two other sharks converged. A feeding frenzy? Would it be painful? Would they take an arm or leg before she drowned? There was a thrashing beneath her, and the big shark shot away like a torpedo fired from a submarine.

The two new sharks came up beside Lola. One had a large dorsal fin. The other was much smaller. Their bottle noses popped out of the water as they chirped and squealed.

Porpoises. Dolphins. A mother and her calf.

Lola turned off the light and swam on her back. She breathed in the love of her newfound friends and exhaled the terror of the big shark. She had heard stories of shipwrecked sailors who had been helped to shore by dolphins. They were swimming beside her, smooth skin against her hand as she stroked. They were guiding her in a certain direction.

LOLA

Against her better judgment, Lola turned on her phone, selected the camera, and raised her arm high enough to include herself and her two friends. She took a picture.

The camera flashed.

The flash frightened the calf. She squealed and swam away, followed closely by her mother. Lola caught a quick glimpse of the picture of the three of them. The screen went black. The phone was dead, and Lola was alive.

Incommunicado was the word that came to mind. She was out of touch with anyone in the real world. Only the unseen world knew of her plight.

She had faith.

The only thing left to do was swim for the shore, that distant blank canvas with a few lights erased by the ghost ship. She knew it would take a long time. She prepared herself mentally. She was a swimmer. She had spent hours doing laps in the pool. The shore could be ten miles away. She could do it. People swam the English Channel. How far was that? She put her dead phone in the back of her tights and wrapped the shirt around her waist in case she needed it later. She began a slow, steady crawl alternating her breathing from side to side.

Practice, practice, practice...

Lola was in a comfortable rhythm until what felt like a knife scratched her cheek. She stopped. She knew what it was.

Jellyfish!

Lola untied the shirt and put her arms in the sleeves that were long enough to cover her hands. She buttoned it up the front to her neck and turned up the collar. Only her face and her feet below the tights were bare. She swam the breaststroke keeping her head above the water. Her feet were stung often, and she absorbed the pain. Each stab propelled her forward.

"I can do this," Lola said

When her neck cramped, she dipped her face into the water with her eyes closed. Underwater, she could hear the sound of an engine. With no boats to be seen, she knew it was the ghost ship without lights. Out of the darkness, the ghost ship came for her.

"Help me, please," Lola yelled.
"Americana," a voice came back.

Four dark arms came down from the side of the big boat as it maneuvered next to her. Two sets of rough hands grabbed each of her wrists and, with a coordinated pull, lifted her out of the water and set her down on a slippery wooden deck. Blinking, she leaned back against the hull and took a deep breath, and held it for a second before she could focus.

She was seated between two men. There was a smell of fish. The engine's sound increased as they turned out to sea.

"We have to clean her up," one of the faces in the dark said.

"We could pee on her like we did when we stepped on a sea urchin or a man of war," the other figure said, laughing.

"Shut up," the other said and smacked him across the back of his head. "Get the ammonia and a clean rag from El Capitano."

"That's what we did when we were boys at the beach," he defended himself as he went away to do what he was told.

When the door to the forward cabin was opened, a red light revealed a dark weathered face beneath a baseball cap. The other

18

came back, a younger worn face with dark curly hair. He carried a plastic bottle of liquid and a rag that he tore in half.

"American," the older said in English and then exchanged some Spanish that made both of them laugh. "I could tell when she yelled. I told you."

The younger man worked on her face with the rag and liquid. He gently removed the tentacles. The man in the ball cap worked on her feet.

Lola smelled the ammonia's strong odor, and it instantly cleared her head.

"I'm Paulie," the young man said. "Who are you, and what are you doing here?"

"I'm Lola," she said. "I fell off of a cruise ship."

"I'm Manuel, the long-haired motherfucker," the man in the cap said. "You have tentacles all over your pants, your shirt, your hair! Ammonia gets rid of the poison, but you have so much. Lay down here. We have to hose you."

"Lay on your back. Close your eyes and mouth. Hold your nose and roll over when I kick you," Paulie said.

"Go get the hose," Manuel said.

Lola did as she was told. Did she have a choice? No.

As she lay on her back, she could feel the ammonia being splashed over her body. Even with her nose closed, she was now dazed by the odor that had once cleared her. Then came the rush from the hose so strong it moved her sideways on the slick deck. She felt a nudge in her side, a soft kick that turned her onto her stomach. Then the splash and flush as they rinsed her legs and buttocks.

"I like your pants," Paulie said as he continued to wash her legs. "I'd like to see them on me."

"Enough," Manuel yelled, and she heard a slap, and the hose stopped.

LOLA

"Never enough," Paulie said, and the two men laughed and did a high five.

Lola sat up and opened her eyes, but all she saw was two pairs of white rubber boots next to her as the two men bent down to help her to her feet that no longer burned from the stings. She tried to see them, but her eyes still blurred, and the light was behind them, so they appeared as shadows, two spirits on a ghost ship.

Lola stood and pulled her arms from their grip. She reached inside her tights and pulled out her cellphone. The light no longer worked. She hoped the pressure hose hadn't damaged it.

"Is that a ten?" Paulie asked. "I only have a seven. Manuel the long-haired motherfucker says he has a ten, but he lies."

"Yes, it's a ten," Lola said. "I took a great picture, but the battery is dead."

The wind was blocked by the main cabin where the red lights still winked and glowed, occasionally blocked by a large man's movement inside.

"Just a while ago?" Manuel asked. "That was the light we saw. We thought it was some new beacon on a lobster trap. El Capitano didn't want to turn around, but we insisted. It has been a bad trip so far. Not many traps. Not many *langostas.*"

"What did El Capitano say when we saw it was a girl?" Paulie asked.

"If she's not big enough, throw her back," Manuel said in a gruff voice. "We don't take any shorts."

Both men laughed out loud.

"Shorts?" Lola said.

"Lobsters that are too small to be legal," Manuel said.

"Legal. Legal," Paulie said. "We only steal legal lobsters."

LOLA

"We are environmental pirates," Manuel said.

Pirates!

Lola shivered. Her tights were a material that dried quickly, but the shirt held water as she remembered her bubble as if it had been ages ago. She looked around on unsteady legs at the slick deck like a dog getting ready to squat. Someone handed her a dry slicker. Then he helped her spread it on the deck, where she sat down.

Lola assumed a lotus position and began to breathe. Her body relaxed. The pain from the jellyfish was gone and now forgotten. Quietly she said a prayer of thanks. One Our Father. One Hail Mary. The Hebrew blessing of the earth. Followed by Inshallah. She wasn't taking any chances with the universe.

"Oooooommmm." Lola released herself from doubt.
"What are you doing?" Paulie said.
"Centering myself," Lola answered.
"You're not afraid?" Manuel said.

"She has nothing to be afraid of," a loud, deep voice came from the lighted cabin that was the wheelhouse. He had a Spanish accent and spoke to the crew in Spanish, but he spoke English when he wanted Lola to understand. He never repeated himself.

"El Capitano," Paulie introduced her to the voice.
"Give the *Langostina* to me," El Capitano told his crew. "She's a keeper."

LOLA

PART TWO

The boat was divided into two parts. Forward was the main cabin that was the wheelhouse and living quarters. Then, the working deck and hatch to the ice hole where the catch was stored. Two large windows overlooked the bow from the wheelhouse, where a sturdy winch held the anchor. Below the windows were the instrument panel and steering station with red lights indicating various functions and the wheel that directed the boat. There were throttle levers by the wheel, and a marine radio turned on.

The man at the wheel was El Capitano, broad and tall in a dirty, faded shirt that at one time may have been brown. His gray hair was thinning and unkempt. His arms were sunburnt and muscular and held tight to the wheel as he shifted his weight from foot to foot. There was a swivel chair behind him that he only used to keep himself standing. When he turned his head to look at Lola, she saw large dark eyes in the same weathered face as the crew. He only glanced at the girl and quickly turned his attention back to the boat and the radio.

The radio bristled with the constant Spanish chatter of a sporting event. There was excitement. There was commentary with competing voices and brief moments of quiet.

LOLA

"*Arriba, arriba,*" was heard again and again. "*Encima de mura.*" Then complete silence.

"It's over the wall," El Capitano said. "A home run."

"Oh, a baseball game," Lola said, standing just inside the cabin door.
El Capitano laughed until he had to stop. There was something wrong. It was him, not the boat.
"Not a game," he said, recovering composure. "A business. The drug business."
"Can't everyone hear them?" Lola said.
"Everyone. The DEA. The Coast Guard. The police. Everyone," he said. "The pirates tell them exactly what is happening. They say You guys have three fast boats tonight. One is in dry dock for repairs. One is just coming out of Government Cut in Miami. One is up by Boca Raton. We have seven boats out tonight. Try to find them on your radar. It's over the wall, homerun! That means the drugs have been delivered. The bad guys win again. Unless you need the drugs. Then the good guys have won. Good guys, bad guys. They are all the same. Men with guns. Men with money. Business as usual. Sometimes they let the DEA catch a boat. They have to give them something. Everybody has to win. Sometimes."

Lola looked around the room. To the right was a galley and table with benches built into the wall. There was a bunk above the table. To the left were two bunks. All around the cabin were windows for a complete view of the boat, including two opening windows by the door that showed the working area of the boat where the crew was playing with their cellphones.

"Can I charge my cellphone?" Lola asked. "I need to call my mother."

LOLA

"Of course," he said and pointed to the side of the instrument panel where there were three USB ports and three cords. "Everybody has a cellphone today. Is that a ten?"

In the glow of the red lights, Lola had a better look at his unshaven graying beard and his red eyes surrounded by black circles. He looked like the devil.

"I only have an old two," he said. He took a phone from one of the four front pockets in his shirt. "I have three daughters. They all have better phones. Look."

He turned on his phone. A picture of three young dark-haired girls and a thin graying woman popped up. They were all smiling.

"Look but don't touch anything," he said. "Just use your phone."

He took her phone and plugged it into one of the ports. Up popped the picture of Lola and the two dolphins. It faded to a charging mode.

"Awesome!" El Capitano said. "Awesome, as the kids all say. Awesome!"

"They are my friends," Lola said. "They saved me from a shark."

"I guess they saved you twice," he said. "The flash. It brought you to me."

"Can I use your phone to call my mother?" Lola said.

"No." He was emphatic. "Not any phone but yours. We aren't supposed to be here. We are pirates."

Lola shivered, and he saw it. He pointed to a blanket on the bunk to the left. She thought about taking off her wet shirt but didn't want to reveal herself.

"The government listens in to all cellphone traffic," he said. "You can call if you have cellular. Our cellular is government-controlled when they let us have it."

24

LOLA

Lola's phone was charged enough to show two bars and no WiFi. It was still plugged in. She took a deep breath and let out a tense exhale. She dialed the number.

"Where have you been?" her mother said before Lola could answer. "Your father said you were with your brother. Your brother said you were with Victor. Who is Victor?"

"I'm alive. I'm safe," Lola said. "I fell off the boat and was saved by these fishermen. I'm on their boat now. It's a long story, and my battery is low."

"A fishing boat!" Her mother went speechless.

El Capitano whispered behind her. "We'll be in port tomorrow."

"We'll be in port tomorrow," Lola said. "I'll tell you the whole story. Don't worry and don't tell anyone. I don't want to get anyone in trouble. Not even Victor. Tell him I'll message him later. I'm fine."

"Who is Victor?" her mother asked.

"The crewman who looks like Dr. Zhivago," Lola said

"Who is Omar Sharif, Alex?" her mother said. "Those big brown eyes!"

Jeopardy. It was a game they played when Lola stayed up late watching old movies and *Jeopardy* while her mother was recovering from her surgery. Her mother would ask, 'who is that actor?' and Lola would look it up on her cellphone. They would watch until the pain medicine kicked in and she could fall asleep. Lola saw that same pained look on the face of El Capitano.

"You're right," Lola said. "Just don't tell anyone what happened to me. It's not a big deal. I'm safe. I will call you from port tomorrow."

"We get off the ship tomorrow," her mother said. "They check all tickets when we leave to make sure everyone returns. You won't be there."

"My ticket is in my backpack," Lola said. "I'm sure you'll think of something."

25

LOLA

El Capitano was giving her a signal to hang up with a finger across his throat.

"You're breaking up," Lola said. "I'm alive. I'm safe."

"What port?" was the last Lola heard before turning off her phone.

"Havana," El Capitano said. "The governments listen to all phone calls. My government. Your government."

"Cuban pirates?" Lola said.

"We are all pirates," he said. "We all have to do something illegal to survive. We take the risk, but you never want to wind up in a Cuban jail."

"What do you do?" Lola asked.

"We take lobsters from traps that don't belong to us," he said. "We sell them to the restaurants who avoid buying from the pirates that overcharge them at the government suppliers. In Cuba, we have equality. Everyone is equally poor. Except for the government. *Patria y muerte.*"

He suddenly stopped talking and leaned over the wheel. She could see that he was in pain. He pushed the throttle forward to increase their speed.

"Are you alright?" Lola moved to help him, but he brushed her away.

"Is nothing." He waited till the spasm passed. "We have good education in Cuba, good doctors. I studied Marine Biology. Paulie is a computer programmer. Manuel is a diver. And we can't support our families. No food. No medicine. Why is the world trying to kill the Cuban people? Politics! Take off that wet shirt. There is a dry blanket on my bunk."

LOLA

Lola took off the wet blue cotton shirt. Her synthetic tights were almost dry. Her sports bra was still damp, as if she had just come from the gym. She could feel the eyes on her from all three men. The crew had come to the cabin door and were looking at her.

"There are good guys and bad guys," El Capitano said, looking at his crew. "And the bad guys are not always the ugly ones."

He closed the door in their faces.

Lola went over to the bunk to the right of the steering station. She wrapped herself in the thin, dry blanket and laid down, feeling the thin rubber mattress. She was exhausted from her adventure. She breathed out the bad and inhaled the good as a curtain of sleep dropped over her. She was alive. Was she safe?

Lola was awakened by the loud roar of a boat. Sirens and then gunfire. She looked around and saw El Capitano was still standing at the wheel. Paulie and Manuel were sitting at the table drinking coffee and jumped up on deck. She knew where she was. She didn't know what was happening.

"Heave to," a voice demanded through a bullhorn over the sound of the roaring engine. Then more gunfire. The roar decreased as it came alongside the fishing boat.

"DEA." Manuel stuck his head inside the cabin.

El Capitano pulled back on the throttle and looked out the window at a speedboat as long as his boat. It was candy apple red with three men in gray uniforms on board. Two men pointed long guns at the crew while the other steered close to them. El Capitano smiled at them and waved as he nudged the wheel closer to them until they fell off but stayed close. The engines of both boats had quieted enough that one of the men could be heard.

"Permission to come aboard?" the sailor asked.

"International waters," Paulie yelled back.

"Just board the fucker," a different man with his gun pointed at the bridge yelled.

The first man put down his gun and ignored him. He was younger and subordinate. He smiled back at Paulie.

"Just a social visit," he said.

The red boat pulled close enough so that the young sailor stepped up on the side of his boat, which was as high as the rail of the fishing boat, and leaped across onto the deck where Paulie and Manuel caught him as he slipped on the deck.

"They call me the Wayward Grouper," the sailor said. "Those other cowboys like playing soldier. I just like the sea."

The Grouper shook hands with Manuel and Paulie, who spoke to each other in Spanish and laughed. He then turned to the cabin where Lola had gotten up and stood next to El Capitano. He patted her on the shoulder.

"*Langostina*, take the wheel," El Capitano told her. "Keep going straight. There are reefs on the other side of their boat. "

El Capitano turned and shook hands with the Grouper.

"Sometimes, I just have to get away from those guys," the grouper said. "What are you up to?"

"Lobsters," El Capitano said. "I have to work to feed my family."

He took out his cellphone and showed the picture of the woman and three girls.

"I have a ten plus." The Grouper slapped a pocket in his shirt. "They look like a nice family. I really don't want to make trouble for you. It's just a job. What have you got in the ice hole?"

"Lobsters," El Capitano said and then to the crew, "Give this young man a few to take home."

Manuel opened the hatch to the ice hole, and Paulie leaned inside and came out with three small tails.

"Shorts?" the Grouper said.

"We don't take shorts," El Capitano said.

"What's under the ice?" the grouper asked as Paulie put the three tails into a plastic bag from inside the hole.

"More ice," El Capitano said and suddenly bent over as a spasm caused him to reach out to Lola to steady himself. She took his hand and squeezed it. Pain was something she had learned about with her mother.

"Where are your badges?" Manuel asked. "Anybody can buy a uniform."

"Badges," the Grouper said with a fake Spanish accent. "We don't need no stinking badges."

"Treasure of the Sierra Madre," Lola said. "Humphrey Bogart, Walter Huston, and Tim Holt."

"You got that right," the grouper said. "But you didn't say it as a question."

"Do you have any pain pills?" Lola asked the Grouper.

"That's what I was going to ask you." He held back a laugh. "And who are you?"

"Lola," she said.

"My niece from Miami." El Capitano had recovered.

"Damn you, Grouper," the bullhorn spoke. "Get your ass back here. There are reefs out here. If we scratch this baby, you'll pay for it. Arrest them or get your ass back here now."

The Grouper stood on the rail of the fishing boat with his catch in the bag.

"There were seven smuggling boats with a load of dope out here last night. We found six of them on the satellite. Nice looking family. Good luck," he said. "I guess you're not one of them."

LOLA

The Grouper stepped from the fishing boat to the red speedboat that took off with a roar and quickly went into the sunrise.

"Where do they get a boat like that?" Paulie said.

"They steal them from the drug smugglers," El Capitano said. He took the wheel back from Lola. She stepped aside and took her blue shirt that was dry and stiff from its hook.

"You could have gone with them," he said.

"I thought you needed help, and I don't like guns," Lola said. She used the shirt to cover her sports bra. It was also long enough to cover her behind. "Do you want to lay down for a while?"

El Capitano said nothing and pushed the throttle forward.

"I have to go to the bathroom," Lola said.

Paulie and Manuel led her out of the cabin past the ice hole to the stern of the boat.

"We use a bucket," Paulie said.

There was an empty white plastic bucket hanging over the side on a rope. He pulled it in and handed it to her. He turned away.

"Better hurry up," Manuel said. "There's a sailboat coming our way."

"I just sit on it?" Lola said. "Can I have some privacy?"

"Of course," Paulie said, and he and Manuel looked away, holding back a laugh. "But first, you have to fill it with water. Just drop it over the side. Hold on to the rope."

Lola took the bucket and held onto the rope. She tossed the empty bucket over the side. It filled with water as the boat drove forward. Suddenly the rope stretched tight from the force of the motion forward, and she was pulled back over the rail into the sea. She hit the water hard. She could hear Paulie and Manuel laughing

LOLA

as the boat pulled away. She was once again in familiar territory. The sea.

She let go of the rope, floated on her back, and relieved herself through her tights. It was only pee. Then she pulled up her shirt, pulled her tights down to her knees, and she pooped in the sea. You had to do what you had to do. The movement of the water cleaned her, and she pulled her tights back up. She saw the bucket behind her and watched it sink.

She kicked herself up to see the fishing boat turning around at the same time a white sailboat motored toward her. Lola treaded water and waited for the fishing boat to reach her. It was a lousy trick they had played on her. She could hear El Capitano cursing his crew in bitter Spanish. The same arms that had rescued her before reached down and lifted her again. The two crewmen wouldn't look her in the eye. They cowered from the anger coming from the wheelhouse. Lola took off the wet shirt and threw it at them. They were rough men, and it was a rough joke. And she had been dumb enough to fall for it. It worked, however. She no longer had to go to the bathroom.

"Have you got any shorts?" someone on the sailboat yelled as they pulled alongside the stalled fishing boat. They put fenders out as they tossed a line to Paulie, who tied it to a cleat. They were tied together as El Capitano urged the boats forward faster.

It was a modest boat with one mast above a cabin set forward with a tiller in the aft cockpit. There were two young men wearing sunglasses. One was large and bearded. The other was small and clean-shaven. Both dressed in colored shorts and T-shirts with an animal logo carrying a football. They looked like a couple of college boys out for a day sail.

"We don't take shorts," El Capitano yelled.

"We have beer," Smaller One said.

31

LOLA

"*Por favor, por favor,*" Manuel and Paulie urged the captain.

"*Rapido.*" El Capitano was irritated. "Make it fast. After what you two did...*rapido! Rapido!*"

Lola watched as Paulie got two small tails from the hole. Manuel took them and leaned down over the side to talk to Smaller One. She couldn't hear what they said. Big Guy went into the cabin and came out with a six-pack and a small plastic bag.

Manuel said something to Paulie, who got a bigger tail and put the six-pack on ice.

"Tonight we party," Paulie said.

Manuel put the plastic bag in his pocket.

All the time, the two men from the sailboat looked at Lola. She looked back without expression.

"How much do you weigh?" Big Guy asked her.

"A hundred pounds soaking wet," she said, looking at Paulie and Manuel.

"*Rapido,*" El Capitano insisted.

"We have a problem." Smaller One looked at Big Guy. "Our mast light is broken, and we need to fix it before dark."

"That's right," Big Guy agreed. "I'm too big for him to pull up, and I hurt my shoulder, so I can't winch him up. Could he just winch you up? It's easy. Just change the bulb. You aren't afraid, are you?"

"Don't do it," Manuel said.

"I can do it," Lola said. She no longer trusted his judgment after the bucket. She was also being a bit spiteful.

Paulie and Manuel stepped aside as the two men on the sailboat helped Lola onto their boat. They maneuvered her over to the mast, where there was a harness that they helped her into. A snap shackle clipped to a metal ring in the center of the harness connected her to a line that led to the top of the mast and back down to the winch for the mainsail. They got close to her and spoke softly as they readied her.

"How did you ever wind up with these guys?" Smaller One asked

"It was an accident," Lola said. "I fell off a boat, and they saved me."

"Saved you for what?" Smaller One scowled.

"Be careful," Big Guy said. "I'm going to put this climber's knot on the rope for the jib so if the main breaks, you'll be safe. You won't fall. You'll just hang there."

"When you get to the top," Smaller One said, "we're going to release the line to their boat and take you with us. We'll take you to Key West."

"What!" Lola was confused. Big Guy had begun to pull her up. Smaller One came up close.

"They not only got beer," Smaller One said. "They also got a pain pill, the kind that puts you to sleep. They put it in your drink, and after ten minutes, you become a party toy. We'll save you."

Lola was on her way up. She was higher than the fishing boat, where she looked down at the crew watching her and El Capitano driving faster, causing the mast to swing wildly, almost striking the wheelhouse. Lola hugged the mast as she reached the top where she could stand on the spreaders that kept cables apart supporting the mast. There was a light at the top and a spinning wind vane. The sailboat steadied as Manuel had Paulie release the two lines that bound the two vessels. They drifted apart, and Big Guy lowered her to the deck and unhooked the harness. She noticed from the sun that they were heading west, not north to the Keys.

LOLA

"You're in good hands now," Smaller One said. "I just never liked the looks of those guys."

Lola looked back at the fishing boat and then at her two new saviors. She had to make a decision fast. The clean-cut drug dealers or the fishermen with a bad sense of humor.

"Don't worry about them," Smaller One said and lifted the front of his shirt. There was a gun in his waistband. The distance between the two boats was increasing.

Lola's second sense kicked in. *The bad guys aren't always the ugly ones.* Without a word, she stepped to the rear of the boat and dove over the side.

"Are you crazy?" Smaller One yelled.

"Don't drink anything," Big Guy yelled after her.

Lola swam as fast as she could as the fishing boat approached. Two sets of strong dark arms reached over the side. She was back on deck.

"This is getting to be a habit," Lola said.

"We're sorry about the bucket," Paulie said. "They did the same thing to me on my first trip."

"Me too," Manuel said. "When I was a boy. 'Our bad' is that how it's said?"

"You're both bad," Lola said. "I came back for my phone."

"*Rapido*," El Capitano yelled.

"He's in a really bad mood," Paulie said. "He's been at that wheel for two days since we had to turn around. He's in a hurry to get home."

"There's no place like home," Lola said.

"*The Wizard of Oz*," Paulie said.

LOLA

"What is *The Wizard of Oz*, Alex?" Manuel said. "*Jeopardy*, right?"

"You get that in Cuba?" Lola asked.

"It is how I learned English in Florida," Manuel said.

"You lived in Florida?"

"It's a long story," Manuel said. "I tell you later. Now we have to catch our dinner."

Lola watched them find a wooden square as large as a big hand, wound vertically with thick plastic line that had a good-sized hook on the end. Paulie reached into the ice hole and took out a fish from among the lobsters. He baited the fish through its mouth and tossed it into their wake until he had unwound enough line for it to skip in and out of the water behind them.

"We could have eaten that fish," Lola said.

"Too old," Manuel said, sniffed the air, and turned up his nose. "Much too old. But good to attract a big fish. At this speed, only a big fish could catch it. You hold one side of the rig with one hand and wrap the line around the frame with the other."

"We could eat lobster," Lola said.

"Not lobster again." The two men laughed. "There is some rice in the galley if you are hungry. No beans. The government doesn't give out beans until next week. "

Lola went into the cabin where El Capitano was still at the wheel. His eyes were redder, and he still swayed from foot to foot. He looked at her and forced a smile.

"I could take the wheel," Lola said. "My father has a boat. He lets me steer. You could get some sleep. Just a nap."

"You have a boat. You go on cruises." El Capitano clicked his tongue. "You are a very rich family. "

LOLA

"Not very rich," Lola said. "My parents spend all their money on vacations when they aren't working. I am lucky to have had a chance to ski, dive, hike, and visit places."

"Lucky *Langostina*," he said. "Will you be lucky for me?"

"Wahoo! Wahoo!" came the voice from the deck. "Come here, Lola. Quick. This is your fish."

"Go," El Capitano said. "Here, wear a hat. Take this one Miami Marlins."

Lola put on the ball cap with the marlin on the front and went back on deck, still in her wet clothes. She looked at the muscles on Manuel's arms bulge as he held the wooden square with the line stretched straight out far back from the boat, where she saw a flash of silver and black lightning leap from the sea. It was magnificent.

"Take the line," Manuel said, handing her the wooden square. She hesitated and looked at Paulie, holding a gaff on a long pole. He winked at her.

"Is this another joke?" Lola said.

"No joke," Manuel said. He moved behind her and reached around her shoulders as he placed the square in her hands, holding it until she had a good grip on one side and holding her by the hips as she was jerked forward by the big fish on the line.

"Do you need help?" Manuel asked as she wiggled out of his grip.

"I can do this," Lola said.

Paulie gave her a pair of worn leather gloves that she put on one hand at a time without losing her grip on the square. She just held it steady while she braced her legs against the rail. The sun was high, and she was sweating under the ball cap. Her arms felt strong as she leaned back against the pull on the line.

LOLA

"Every time he jumps, you wrap a handful of line around the square," Manuel said. "If you get tired, I'll take it."

"I can do this by myself," Lola said, and she took two wraps around the square when the fish came out of the water and splashed into the wake of the boat. The boat moving forward faster, pulled the fish so it couldn't dive. It jumped again, and she took two more turns on the line.

"Keep it tight," Paulie said, standing at her shoulder close enough for her to feel his breath on her cheek. "*Chicita forte*. Strong. The way I like a woman."

"Strong enough to kick you out," Manuel said.

"She didn't kick me out," Paulie said. "I left her. I was too much man for her."

"Keep your mind on the fish," Lola said.

"His wife threw him out," Manuel said. "He didn't make enough money to take care of her and two babies."

"Three babies," Paulie said. "I am much man."

"This was harder than I thought," Lola said as her arms began to cramp. The fish was close to the back of the boat. Manuel put his hands on her waist and moved her to the side of the boat out of the wake.

"Get the gaff!" Manuel said.

The large metal hook on the end of the gaff reflected the sunlight. Paulie leaned in close to her as she wrapped the line enough to pull the head of the fish out of the water. In one quick swipe, he swung the hook under the mouth of the fish and lifted it out of the water and onto the deck as Lola sat down with the square still in the frozen grip of her hands that trembled up her arms to shoulders. Her legs stretched out in front of her spasmed as she relaxed her muscles. Her ball cap was stained wet. She was sweating from every pore in her body, through her shirt, through her tights.

37

LOLA

Manuel pried her hands loose from the square and peeled off the wet leather gloves. She took long deep breaths.

"I did it." Lola laughed in a halting breath.

"You look like you could use a shower," Paulie said. "Get the hose."

"Viva Langostina," El Capitano yelled from the wheelhouse.

"You owe us a bucket," Manuel said and patted her on her shaking shoulder.

Lola looked at the fish.

The fish was on the deck next to her. He was as tired as she was. He was almost as long as she was. Its mouth opened wide, revealing rows of short sharp teeth in its upper and lower jaw and the hook caught in the side of his mouth. It was gasping for air, its gills opening and closing. Its crescent-shaped tail flapped and lay down.

"He's beautiful," Lola said.

"Ten kilos," Paulie said.

From the tip of his pointed snout to the base of his black tail, there were waves of white stripes over a black, blue, or green body, depending on how the light hit it. There were flashes of silver.

"Throw him back," Lola said. The wavy stripes made him look like he was still in the water. That was where he belonged.

"No," Pauie said. *"Chica loca."*

"Langostina..." El Capitano started to speak but stopped. Another spasm.

"It's her fish," Manuel said. "She caught it."

"It's my fish," Lola insisted. It was long and lean like her. It was muscular and wanted to live.

LOLA

"Throw him back," Lola said.

Paulie put on the leather gloves, held the lower jaw, and cut the line at the hook with his belt knife.

"The hook," Lola said.

"It will rust out later," Paulie said.

He lifted the fish in both arms and lowered him into the water, facing forward so that water came through its mouth and over his gills. With a whip of his tail, the fish turned and was gone.

They watched him swim to freedom. At a safe distance, the fish jumped high out of the sea and twisted his body in a wave goodbye. Lola waved back and looked at Paulie and Manuel, who did the same but with less enthusiasm.

"You owe us a bucket and a fish dinner," Manuel said.

"Oh, no," Paulie said, "not lobster again tonight."

"With a cold beer," Manuel reminded him.

"Oh, yes," Paulie said. "Tonight we party."

"Why did you come back?" Manuel asked Lola.

They were sitting on top of the hatch to the ice hole, sucking on pieces of ice that tasted like fish. Lola didn't mind. It was cold, and for all she knew, it was clean. Paulie offered her a plastic cup of water from the galley, but she refused.

"My father taught me how to navigate," Lola said. "The sun comes up in the east. It goes down in the west. So," she pointed, "that way is north. We are headed south. They said they were going to take me to Key West. That's north. They headed west. I got an 'A' in geography."

"You're a smart girl," Manuel said. "But when we get to Cuba, maybe too smart for your own good."

"How's that?" Lola said.

39

LOLA

"You have no passport. No identification card. They could throw you into a Cuban jail. That is the last thing you would want," Manuel said.

"I see," Lola said. "Why can't I just go to the American embassy?"

"Without papers, you could never get past the spies that watch the Consulate. I don't know if you have an embassy this year. One year we are America's friend. The next administration says we are the enemy. The next, we are friends again. Then again, we are the enemy. Then you are the enemy. Then you are welcome to come visit and spend money, but not dollars. Euros. Pesos. But you can send dollars to relatives who have to convert them to *cukes*, Cuban pesos, at the government exchange where they take their cut. It is all very confusing."

"Sometimes the magic works, sometimes it doesn't," Lola said.

"Little Big Man," Manuel answered. "What is Little Big Man, Alex?"

"Correct," Lola said. "You must have watched a lot of American TV."

"I had plenty of time," Manuel said. "I was in an American jail for two years."

Paulie came out of the cabin with a big bowl of rice and pieces of pan-fried lobster. He offered it to Lola first in one of three small plastic bowls that needed to be washed. She hesitated.

"You must be hungry after that fish," Paulie said. "I'm sorry for the bowl, but freshwater is valuable out here."

"And the service is terrible." Manuel scooped some food from the big bowl with a small bowl and began to eat with his fingers. "It is really very good. Paulie is a chef. He worked for Royal Castle when he was in Miami."

LOLA

"That must have been a long time ago," Lola said. 'they are all gone now."

"Back in the day when you had 'wet foot, dry foot," Manuel said.

"Eat, *chicita*." Paulie dipped out a small bowl for her.

"I don't know if I can trust you," Lola said.

"No tricks," Paulie said, and he and Manuel looked at each other without smiling.

"They said they sold you some pain pills that would put me to sleep in ten minutes," Lola said.

"What do we look like to you?" Paulie said.

"A couple of pirates," Lola said flatly.

Paulie and Manuel laughed and shared a high five.

"And what do I look like to you?" Lola was serious.

"You are a beautiful woman," Manuel said, and Paulie agreed.

"You men are all alike," Lola said. "Let me see if my cellphone is charged."

She went into the cabin where El Capitano was still at the wheel. He seemed much more at ease. He handed Lola an empty plastic bowl. He yawned.

"Please have Manuel come take the wheel," he said. "I have to lay down. Tell him to anchor at the usual place."

He turned to the nearby bunk and fell into it. He let out a loud yawn and was asleep before he hit the mattress. Manuel was already at the wheel.

"Sometimes the magic works," Manuel said to Lola.

She looked at him and gave a high five.

The sun was setting behind the skyline of Havana off to the right as Paulie set the anchor in a small cove. He got the beer out of the hole, gave two to Manuel, and offered one to Lola, who refused but accepted a chunk of fishy ice. She noticed the large white scar on the back of Paulie's wrist as he handed it to her. He saw where her eyes went and held it up for her to see better in the fading daylight.

"Barracuda," Paulie said and opened the can of beer and swallowed it whole before opening the next one. "I was spearfishing and was wearing a large silver watch that a Canadian had left behind."

"He left it in Paulie's pocket." Manuel laughed as he finished a beer and was about to throw it overboard.

"Please don't do that," Lola said.

"It's a home for some small fish," Manuel said.

"It's pollution," Lola said.

He found a tattered sack near the cabin and placed the can inside. Then he gave the sack to Paulie, who did the same with his two empty cans.

"Okay?" he asked Lola.

"Thank you," she said.

"Should we save the other two beers for El Capitano?" Paulie asked.

"No," Manuel said and got the rest of the beer. "He'll be asleep for hours."

The inside of the cabin was dark. With the engine turned off, not even the red instruments glowed. They could hear snoring. Lola found her phone and took it back on deck.

"Have you got some good music on there?" Paulie asked as he stood up and started to dance with himself. "It's party time."

"I have Bruno Mars," Lola said. "I hope I have enough bars on my phone."

Lola turned on her phone.

"OMG," she said. "I have an email from my mother."

"Read it to us, is okay?" Manuel said.

LOLA

Lola read, "We're in the car. Where are you? I wore a tank top with no bra when we disembarked, so no one looked at your ticket when it was scanned. Ha Ha."

"I like your mother," Paulie said, and Manuel playfully slapped him on the shoulder.

Lola continued, "They just called me on my phone to make sure I got off. I told them that the scanner malfunctioned. They said the attendant remembered me. Ha Ha. They apologized."

Both Paulie and Manuel laughed as they finished another beer and put the cans in the sack.

"Is there more?" Paulie asked.

Lola read slowly, "We spent most of the day in the lounge watching TV. The cone of uncertainty. There is a hurricane coming. Write when you get work. Ha Ha! M&D."

LOLA

PART THREE

It all happened at once. The thunder. The lightning. The scream. The downpour.

Lola's phone went blank, eliminating the only light on deck. The thunder rolled across the sea and rocked the boat. The lightning flash was so bright she could see the white sand on a small beach and the green jungle behind it. The scream came from El Capitano as he came out of the cabin with a bowl in his hand and a smile on his face. He threw the bowl, and whatever was in it into the sea. The sky opened up, and rain fell in torrents from the black sky.

Paulie and Manuel each took an arm of El Capitano, whose pants were down around his ankles, and danced in a circle, looking up at the heavens with their mouths open catching the rain. They were laughing so hard they almost choked. They took off their white rubber boots and splashed in the water pooling on the deck. They were a little bit drunk, except for El Capitano, who saw Lola as he turned and quickly pulled up his pants. He took Lola by both hands and pulled her into the rain dance.

"My lucky *Langostina*," El Capitano said. "I plssed it. I passed it, and I'm a lucky bastit.

Lola wasn't sure what to make of his sudden jubilation.

"The kidney stone!" he yelled. "I am a man again. *Patria y Vida!*"

He let go of her hands, and Lola looked up into the downpour that washed over her, taking away the salt from her stiff clothes and matted hair. Paulie ran his fingers through his curls, but Manuel kept his cap on. As suddenly as the rain had started, it stopped.

El Capitano took Lola inside the cabin and closed the door

"Take off your clothes," El Capitano said once they were inside. "Wrap the blanket around you and dry off. Your feet. You have been wet too long. We have to get you some shoes. I'll run the engine tonight and put your clothes over it so they will be dry in the morning when you walk the *Malecon*. We can't have you looking like a pirate. You have to look like a tourist. That way, the police will leave you alone. Sleep in my bunk tonight. Be rested. It will be a difficult day tomorrow. We have to get you off of the boat before the police come."

Lola was clean and warm and safe inside the blanket as she fell into the darkened bunk where sleep came as suddenly as the rain.

Lola woke up to find her clothes neatly folded at the foot of the bunk. The cabin door was open, and she could see the three men on deck. Beyond them were the dock and a marina with many shops. She could hear El Capitano giving orders to the crew.

LOLA

"Paulie," he yelled, "go to the store and get a big pair of sunglasses and an ass pack."

"Butt pack." Manuel laughed.

"Fanny pack," Lola said as she came out on deck wrapped in the blanket.

"Fanny pack, yes," El Capitano said. "And a big straw hat."

"*Si*," Paulie said and was off on his mission.

"Manuel," El Capitano said. "There is a beautiful aloe plant next to that shop. Cut a leaf for me. Lagostina, sit on the hatch and wipe off your feet."

Lola's feet were wet from the deck again, and the soles had turned white and shriveled. She hadn't noticed it before, having spent most of her life shoeless or in water, but they returned to normal once they were dry and in socks or sandals. Now she had no shoes.

Manuel gave a spear of aloe to El Capitano, who split it open with the nails of his thumbs and rubbed the liquid from the inside between his palms. He started to bend down through the stiffness in his back. He stopped. He motioned for her to raise her feet while keeping the blanket tucked between her legs. He handed the aloe to Manuel and pointed to Lola's feet.

"I'll do that," Paulie said as he came back onto the deck. He dropped a large straw hat with a pair of sunglasses and a fanny pack inside next to Lola.

"Did you give her the presents?" Paul asked.

"Not yet," Manuel said and gave up the aloe and looked into the straw hat.

"No receipt?"

"Someone left them at the restaurant," Paulie said. He knelt and rubbed the juice from the plant on Lola's feet. He was gentle and

46

thorough. He continually smiled at her. "People get drunk and forget things all the time."

"Enough is enough," El Capitano said and pulled him up by his curly hair.

"Thank you so much," Lola said. "It feels so good. I could go dancing."

"You might need shoes," Paulie said, and he winked at Manuel.

"*Viva zapatos*," Manuel said and lifted the sack that contained the empty beer cans. He took out a pair of rope sandals. One was larger than the other, one had a strap across the back, and one had a rope across the ankle. Both had a piece of leather sewn across the front.

"We were up all night making these." Paulie was proud. "I made the right. Manuel, the long-haired motherfucker, made the left."

Lola leaned forward, keeping herself wrapped, and with Paulie's help, got her feet onto the rope soles sewn in tight circles. Paulie helped with the straps and massaged her calf.

"Now," El Capitano said. "Put on your clothes and go."

Lola picked up the hat and put it on. She took the sunglasses out. She examined the pack and found some money folded inside. She read the 'Gucci' brand on the glasses. 'Versace' was printed on the pack.

When Lola put them on and looked around, she saw a man in a green uniform coming from behind one of the buildings zipping up the front of his pants.

"El Capitano," the policeman called to them. "*Que pasa, amigo*?"

"Diego," El Capitano greeted the policeman.

"*Permisso*?" Diego hesitated before he came on board.

LOLA

"*Si*," El Capitano said, and he gave him a hand crossing the rail. The cop was heavy and wore a belt with a gun and a radio. He held the breast pocket of his shirt to secure his cellphone.

"It was a quick trip," the policeman said.

Lola backed away against the far rail with Paulie and Manuel. Her hat pulled down over her face as they interpreted the Spanish the two men spoke when she looked at them.

"I had to turn around," El Capitano said. "I was passing a kidney stone. I screamed like a baby. I wouldn't wish such a thing on my worst enemy."

"So you came back with what you had when you left?" the cop said. "*Nada?*"

"A few lobsters," El Capitano said.

The cop walked around the deck looking at nothing in particular until he saw the sack with the empty beer cans. He picked it up and looked inside. He emptied the cans onto the deck.

"Where did you get this illegal red, white, and blue beer? This could be evidence," Diego said.

"Are you going to arrest me or seize my boat?" El Capitano said. He laughed. "The paperwork would ruin a fine day with a hurricane coming. I'm sure we both have to get ready."

"The state owns your boat," the cop said. "I am only a public servant looking out for the people's property."

They both looked up at a darkening sky.

Paulie came over and started putting the cans back in the sack.

"*Una momento*," the cop said. "Did you get any lobsters?"

"A few," Paulie said.

"Enough to fill that sack?" the cop asked.

Paulie took the sack and emptied the cans over the side.

LOLA

"No!" Lola reacted without thinking.

"No?" the policeman said and looked closely at her wrapped in the blanket and under the hat with her head down, looking at her mismatched sandals. "*Como se llama?*"

Lola had picked up enough Spanish in her life that she knew that he was asking her name.

"*Langostina,*" Lola said.

Paulie and Manuel laughed.

"My daughter," El Capitano said and took out his cellphone. "Here, look at this picture of my family from a few years ago. She has grown so much you wouldn't recognize her." Then he whispered. "*Ella es Autista.*"

The cop stepped back as if he had seen a snake and quickly pulled his cellphone from his shirt pocket.

"*Mira,*" he said. "My family. The boy is now a doctor, and my daughter is studying chemistry. We all have family. Mouths to feed."

There was a clap of thunder, and rain began to fall.

El Capitano pushed Lola inside but left the cabin door open so the cop could see inside. He motioned Paulie to the ice hole and directed Manuel to do what he had to do.

"Fill the sack," he said. "And Manuel, add some of the ice. Use a shovel."

"*Langostina!*" The policeman laughed. "Keep a few for yourself. We all have to eat."

The sack was full, and Manuel dug a large shovel of ice to put on top. The cop inspected the contents, hefted it, and carried it to the rail. He looked back inside the cabin before he stepped back onto the dock and the rain increased.

"I hope you have better luck next time, *amigo,*" he said and then looked at Paulie. "I won't mention the destruction of evidence."

LOLA

They all laughed with him as he ran off behind a shop out of the rain. It was a passing shower. Lola came to the door. They nodded that it was okay to come out.

"We have to get you away now," El Capitano told her and hugged her. "*Langostina*, my lucky *Langostina*. Manuel take her to the *Malecon*."

"I can do it," Paulie said. "Manuel gave Diego everything. I kept a few lobsters for us."

"He'll sell what he got to the restaurants. I need you here to get ready for the storm. You gave him everything." El Capitano looked up at a clearing sky.

"Everything," Paulie assured him.

"I wish I could take a picture of all of you with my phone," Lola said.

"No pictures, please," El Capitano said. "And don't remember any names or the boat. If anyone should stop you, tell them you are Canadian."

The *Malecon* was a seawall miles long on the Havana waterfront. It had a wide walkway between the wall and six lanes of light traffic early in the morning. Lola and Manuel had walked through awakening neighborhoods with the strong smell of coffee and streets empty of trash.

"It's so clean," Lola said.

"Cubans have no trash," Manuel told her. "They can't afford to waste anything."

He was dressed in torn jeans and a faded shirt open down his chest, revealing his dark brown skin marked with several white scars. Instead of his white rubber boots, he wore a pair of thin rubber flip-flops. He still wore his baseball cap.

LOLA

Lola was no different than the other tourists they passed. Large hat, sunglasses, and a pack worn in the back or front. The women wore shorts or tights and sneakers or sandals.

The further they walked, the more people they saw strolling or going. The younger Cubans dressed more like American teens except for the children in school uniforms that hurried along laughing and displaying cellphone images or messages as they carried backpacks full of school materials.

"Over there is the American consulate." Manuel pointed to an unremarkable tan building across the highway among the rows of old pastel-colored buildings at various stages of decay or reconstruction. "See the policemen at the corners. You would have to go by them to get in, and you have no papers. They would call on their radios, and more police would come to take you away."

There were people setting up small vending stations along the seawall. A few fishermen had cast lines into the bay. Across the water in the distance was a lighthouse and a fort. Everyone kept looking up at the clouds that shrouded the sunrise. The wind had increased, and some of the sellers retreated away from waves that now splashed up over the wall.

"The *Hotel Nationale*," Manuel said. He pointed to a large white building. "All of the important visitors stay there."

"Important?" Lola smiled.

"Money," Manuel said. "Who was the richest man in the world before the revolution?"

"That's before I was born," Lola said.

"A Cuban," Manuel said. "A billionaire when people only wanted to become millionaires. Who was Julio Lobo, Alex?"

"Never heard of him," Lola said.

51

LOLA

"He was the sugar king," Manuel said. "Sugar, the world's drug of choice. He controlled the world's market for the sweet addiction. "

"What happened to him?" Lola asked.

"He got old and died." Manuel laughed. "Just like the poorest man in the world. But his money did get him the chance to grow old while others of lesser money were executed."

"What about you?" she asked. "Do you have enough money to grow old?"

"I don't need money," Manuel said. "I have a skill."

"You're a fisherman," Lola guessed.

"I am a welder." Manuel stuck out his scarred chest. "They need me."

"To build a better future?" Lola said.

"To cut holes in the bottom of boats." Manuel stopped. He bought some *tacitos* from a woman before running from the incoming sea.

They sat along the seawall sideways with an eye on the tide and jumped out of the way of incoming, laughing when they got splashed but not soaked. Lola almost tripped over her sandals. She took them off when they sat back down and tucked them inside the belt of her 'Versace' fanny pack. She noticed that some sellers also had designer packs and her 'Gucci' sunglasses.

"All fakes," Manuel told her. "Commerce. Money. Lies."

"It's all illegal," Lola said.

"Illegal? No. Commerce," Manuel said. "Like stolen lobsters. Illegal is whenever the state doesn't get its share. Remember the Grouper from the red boat. He said they found six of the seven drug boats. We were the seventh boat."

LOLA

"You were smuggling drugs." Lola understood. "But El Capitano had to turn around too soon because of his kidney stone."

"Not exactly," Manuel explained. "Remember the sailboat. We were supposed to trade our goods for cash that we would smuggle back into Cuba."

"But the deal was blown," Lola said, "when they tried to save me."

"Or they didn't want any witnesses," Manuel said, and a chill ran through Lola as a wave caught her from the side, and neither of them laughed. Manuel had jumped out of the way.

"We have time," he said, watching the line of vintage cars lining up along the *Malecon*.

"I tell you a story. Wet foot, dry foot. When Cubans tried to escape to America, if the police caught you in the water, they sent you back to Cuba. If they caught you on US soil, you were safe to become an American. Wet foot, dry foot. That was the law. Paulie and I were kids. We found an old boat and sailed off into the Gulf. The boat sank, and we held onto empty water jugs for two days before a helicopter going to an oil rig found us and took us to the refinery, where we stepped onto dry land and became Americans. I worked dirty jobs and learned welding. Pauli worked in the cafeteria and studied computers. We wanted to get back to Cuba. You have to understand all Cubans love Cuba. They just don't like governments. We found a boat that belonged to the oil company, and then they found us and sent us to Miami to go to jail. For two years, they kept us waiting. Then they let us go for lack of evidence. In jail, we met some drug smugglers who gave us the name of a man who needed workers. Paulie sat in an old apartment on the Miami River and kept track of the boats coming in, some ours, some for the DEA to keep them happy. The boats that were ours needed someone to cut holes in the hulls to get out the hidden drugs and then patch up the hole.

LOLA

When other boats went by on the river, my boat would bounce up and down, so I had to dig a hole underneath to crawl in so I wouldn't get crushed. I put on a dive tank and delivered the goods to a parking lot at a shopping center with my new skills. And that is how the big banks, hotels, and apartment buildings were financed. A bank on every corner."

"And you still are smuggling drugs." Lola was judgmental.

"Commerce," Manuel said. "Demand and supply. We smuggle dollars into Cuba for the people, and the state gets its share. Remember Diego, the cop. He was there to pick up the money for the state. I gave him back the drugs with the lobsters. Who knows what he will do with it. But the real reason we do it is that we love the sea."

"There is just one more question I wanted to ask you," Lola said.

"Here comes your ride," Manuel said and started to walk away. "His name is Jose. Just tell him you are a friend of Manuel, the long-haired motherfucker."

Lola saw a green convertible stop on the *Malecon*. She turned to see Manuel blow her a kiss and turn away. He took off his baseball cap, and a braided ponytail unwound down to his butt, fanny, ass. He did a little sidestep to make it swing back and forth.

"That was my question, and what does he do with it?" Lola said to herself, and she couldn't stop laughing until she heard a familiar voice.

"Excuse, please," Diego said in English, pulling up his gun belt. He had a green poncho that he wore as a cape but pulled it around to cover his shirt and belt. The rain had increased but was not overwhelming. He saw she was getting wet as she pulled her long-sleeved shirt down over her 'Versace' pack and one of the rope sandals fell out of the belt. He picked up the sandal and inspected it.

"Can I help you?" Lola said from under her wide-brimmed hat.

"What is your name?" Diego asked in English.

"Lola," she said. "I am Canadian."

"Can I see your identification, please?" he said.

"I left it at the Hotel Nationale with my parents," she said.

"And the last name?"

"Lobo," she said.

"*Rico que Lobo*." He laughed and then, in English, said, "Rich as Lobo!"

Lola was getting wet, and she could see the man in the green convertible putting up the top. The wind was pushing the waves over the seawall. Everyone was heading for cover.

"Every Cuban's dream is to be rich as Lobo." He walked around her, so his body shielded her from the spray. He looked down at her bare feet. He slapped the sandal against the palm of his hand.

"Punked! That is what my children call it. And my old friend El Capitano. He punked me, *Langostina*."

"You speak very good English," Lola said.

"We have very good schools in Cuba," he said and added, "for everyone."

"I just want to call my parents and let them know I'm alright," Lola said and took her waterproof cellphone from her pack.

"That looks like a new one," he said, "A ten plus?"

"No, just a ten," Lola said. "Can I make a call?"

"Not here," Diego said. "I am supposed to evacuate the *Malecon*. A hurricane is coming spawning tornados. They expect a tidal wave, but it is still in the cone of uncertainty. You go, *Langostina*.

El Capitano will explain it all to me later. I don't have any idea of what to do with you now. Maybe I will see you later at the hotel. Let me take your picture."

He found his cellphone under the poncho and pointed at Lola, rain obscuring the lens. He quickly put it back under cover. He took her cellphone. She had turned it on to call. He pressed the icon for photos. Up popped the picture of Lola and the dolphins.

"Awesome!" Diego laughed. "Awesome, correct? No pictures of El Capitano's boat."

He gave her back her phone and her sandal.

"*Patria y vida*," Lola said.

"But not so loud," Diego said over the wind. "*Adios, Langostina*. You are a very beautiful woman."

Lola rolled her eyes. He was gone somewhere behind her. She headed for the green car with the passenger door open. The wind slammed it shut behind her.

"Jose?" she said and took off her 'Gucci' glasses and wiped the rain from her eyes with a damp shirt sleeve. "I am a friend of Manuel the..."

"Long-haired motherfucker," Jose said and extended a wet hand that she shook. "*Patria y vida!*"

"You speak English?" Lola asked.

"English, French, German, and *poco Italiano*," Jose said. He drove onto the highway and then turned down a narrow side street. Even in the rain, people were lined up along the sidewalk on the leeward side of the rows of old buildings.

Two policemen in green uniforms were on each corner, more concerned with an argument accentuated by a throwing motion and a bat swing.

LOLA

"Baseball." Jose saw her watching. "More important than hurricanes or potatoes."

"Potatoes?" Lola said.

"The potato truck came in yesterday," Jose said. "That's why the people are lined up even in a storm to get their ration of potatoes. We are a poor country, but we love it. If it was legal, every Cuban in Miami would come home to Cuba. This is paradise. Except for an occasional hurricane or a revolution."

"Is the hurricane really coming here?" Lola asked.

"Yes," Jose said. "And so is the revolution. Not with guns but with this."

He showed her his cellphone.

"I have to call my mother," Lola said.

"I know a place where there is internet today," Jose said. "Because of the storm. It is like electricity. Some days we have it. Some days we cook with charcoal. It's all good."

The rain had stopped. There was a stillness in the air. The calm before the storm.

Jose parked the car on a vacant sidewalk on a side street near a church at the end of an open courtyard with a large tree in the middle surrounded by benches. A few people were headed to the impressive spired old church. The crowds filled the benches around the tree. Each person had a cellphone. It was a hot spot.

"You can't call, but you can send emails on certain days." Jose opened her door and led her closer to the tree. "This is the day."

Lola opened her phone and saw an email from her mother.

WE WERE ABLE TO TRACK YOUR PHONE TO CUBA. DAD HEARD FROM AN OLD AIR FORCE BUDDY IN MIAMI THAT THEIR SPY HAD TOLD OUR SPY THAT YOU WERE LAST SEEN ACROSS FROM THE US CONSUL WITH A FISHERMAN KNOWN AS MANUEL THE LONG-HAIRED MOTHERFUCKER.

LOLA

PART FOUR

Lola started to laugh and cry at the same time. She wrote a reply. The rain was returning.

I'M ALIVE. I'M SAFE. THE CUBAN PEOPLE ARE THE NICEST PEOPLE I HAVE EVER MET. I WILL BE HOME AFTER THE STORM. LOVE YOU. MISS YOU ALL HERE COMES THE RAIN. THANK YOU SO MUCH FOR THE WATERPROOF CASE FOR MY PHONE. IT'S A TEN. HAHA, TELL YOU THE JOKE WHEN I SEE YOU.

LOL LOLA.

She pushed the send button and heard the swoosh. Delivered.

The rain was coming through in bands. A line of showers and wind followed by periods of clear skies. People behaved accordingly in and out of doorways but still retained a place in the potato line. The internet had been cut off, so the people dispersed. There were pairs of policemen in every direction more intent on the swift-moving clouds than the baseball.

Lola and Jose rode with the top down during a passing calm. The breeze created by their movement alleviated the thickness of the humidity. They stopped in front of a building with a crumbling facade .

"I want you to meet my wife," Jose said. "And maybe we can get you into some Cuban clothes. You don't want to look like a tourist.

We have a long road ahead of the storm. We don't want to be here if there is a tidal wave."

"Where are we going?" Lola asked.

"To the other side of the island to my father's house where we will be safe."

They secured the top and rolled up the windows of the old Ford. Lola stopped to look it over. She turned to Jose.

"I think this is my grandfather's old car," Lola said. "He always talks about his Ford Sunliner convertible in Miami when he was in the Air Force at Homestead Air Base during the Cuban missile crisis."

"The Russian missile crisis," Jose corrected her. "It was the Russians who had the missiles, not the Cubans. He must be like my father, an old warrior."

"He says he was in the Cold War," Lola said. "The one we won."

Jose laughed as they entered a large, heavy wooden door. There was a foyer where a woman greeted him. A man patted him on the back and whispered, "*Patria y vida.*"

They walked down a narrow corridor with apartments on each side. It was freshly painted and clean. That stopped at an open door.

"This is Lola," Jose said. "My wife, Maria."

A woman in a fresh dress with her black hair streaked with silver neatly combed met them with a smile and a hug for each of them.

Inside was a living room and dining room with a kitchen to one side and doors leading to other rooms further back. It was neat and clean furnished as apartments that Lola had been in back home. It was colorful comfort. There was a picture of Fidel Castro next to one of Che on the wall behind a television. There were flowers in a vase on the dining room table. They looked real.

LOLA

"We have to get you into some clothes," Jose said and conferred with his wife.

"Our daughter Juanita is sheltering at the school. She is about your size," Jose told Lola with his wife's consent. "You can take a quick shower if we have water today. It's in her room. Maria will set out a school uniform on the bed. Just leave your clothes in the bathroom, a fair exchange. No?"

"Yes," Lola said. "But not my big brother's shirt. It has sentimental value."

The shower was cold without much pressure. She smiled when she remembered the rain shower on the boat. She suddenly felt like dancing. She looked down at her feet that had resumed their natural color after the aloe treatment. There was something red on her foot.

Blood! The curse.

"Oh, no!" Lola said out loud, and Maria came to see the reason.

"Aye, aye, aye," Maria said. "It is cool. Cool? Is right? On the trip, you help me with my English. I get you the tampon. Tampon is universal for common problem but not easy to find in Cuba. *Touristas* leave them for us. Gratuity. Is good?"

Lola wore a mustard-colored jumper with a white shirt and a blue scarf around her neck. She wore knee-high white socks and her rope sandals. Her big brother's blue shirt was tucked under her in the backseat, where she sat with Maria, who had a list to be translated. Jose drove slowly through the streets filled with people seeking safety from the storm.

The world was under gray clouds over gray buildings until they got to the main highway. It was like any other highway. Six concrete lanes and a few overpasses sheltered some from the downpours.

LOLA

There were merging lanes and dividing lines that led to a four-lane freeway that extended in a direct line away from the city into the surrounding farmlands and cane fields and the next band of showers and wind.

Jose was quietly driving until the light traffic spaced itself to red tail lights far in front and headlights disappearing behind them. Lola and Maria sat on opposite sides of the backseat. They leaned in closer when the sound of the rain and wind drowned out their voices.

"My English lesson," Maria said and looked at her list. "I first, and you translate."

"*Si,*" Lola said.

"BFF," Maria said.

"BFF?" Lola was surprised and then comprehended. "BFF, best friends forever."

"Best friends forever," Maria repeated. "FYI?"

"For your information," Lola said.

"For your information," Maria repeated slowly. "TMI?"

"Too much information." Lola smiled and played the game.

"LOL," was the next word.

"That's a good one," Lola thought out loud. "LOL, lots of love, lots of luck, lots of laughs. Laugh out loud."

"TMI, TMI." Maria laughed. "I am a techie, yes?"

"*Si,*" Lola said

"One more," Maria said. WTF?"

"What the..." Lola stopped and saw that Jose was listening.

"FUCK!" Jose shouted, "Get down. Cover your faces!"

"What's wrong?" Lola had to yell over the seat into his ear to be heard above the sound of an approaching train. Jose pushed her back and stopped the car, laying down across the front bench seat as the noise grew so loud it rattled the car, and the side windows shattered. Lola looked up to see the convertible's ragtop spread its wings and fly into the swirling gray sky. Then the train hit, spinning the car around and around before it settled, and she looked up and could see through the shattered window the black cone of a tornado rising back up into the gray sky.

Lola looked at Jose as he sat up and turned to look at his glass-covered passengers.

"OMG," they both said at the same time and watched Maria shake glass from her hair.

"OMG?" Maria said.

"Oh, my God," Lola told her.

"OMG," Maria said. "WTF!"

They all laughed and exhaled, looking up at the sky that now showed patches of blue. Jose looked at the highway that led into the blackness in both directions. He was unsure. The car rested sideways across two lanes. There were no other cars in sight. The sun blinked out for a second, long enough to cast a shadow.

"Is it afternoon?" Lola asked him.

"Two o'clock," he said.

"That way," Lola said and pointed into one blackness. "We were going south. That way. I got an 'A' in geography and have navigation experience. FYI."

Lola raised her hand, and from the backseat, Maria slapped it.

"BFF, high five," Maria said. "OMG, I'm a techie."

They all looked out at the cane fields that had been flattened. Far to one side, a large cloth waved to them. It was the blown-away ragtop. All three trekked carefully over the cane mat, slipping and sliding until they reached the convertible top that was still intact but heavy with water. It took all three of them tugging and lifting to get it back to the car and then up onto the metal frame from which it had fled.

Jose fitted the front into the windshield and clamped it down beneath the metal strip that had held it in place. The plastic window in the back of the top was creased and scratched to obscure visibility, but it would still keep the rain out. Jose found enough rope in the trunk to tie the wings to the door frames. They had to climb through the shattered side windows to get back in the car. Maria brushed away enough glass from the seat to be able to lay down with her face below the front seats out of the wind as Jose started the engine.

"Ford, straight-six engine." Jose smiled. "Best they ever made. And easy to repair or replace."

Lola sat in the front seat with him. She looked at his profile as he returned to their journey. He was an ageless man with a distinctive nose and proud chin. His eyes were bright with anticipation. His wet black hair was matted with curling gray sideburns. He had a large forehead with rows of creases. A neat black mustache accented his ever-present smile. He was handsome. Lola had to look away as their speed increased wind watered her eyes. She ducked beneath the windshield with her chin on the dashboard. The rearview mirror had survived with a religious medal still dangling and swaying.

"Saint Christopher? " Lola said.

"What?" Jose said. "Louder. The wind is in my ears."

Lola looked in the backseat and saw that Maria was resting. How could she sleep? They were in the midst of disaster.

"Saint Christopher!" Lola yelled.

"*Si*," Jose said. "I will take any help I can get."

"Are you religious?" Lola asked, finding an audible level by leaning next to him without shouting.

"Isn't it wonderful?" He laughed. "Look at what nature can do. The wind. The rain. The storm. It is alive. We are alive."

He suddenly slowed the car.

LOLA

"Checkpoint," Jose said. "Lay down with your head against the door. Don't look around. Don't say anything."

They stopped at a barrier, a red and white arm that had been lowered in front of them. A small wooden guardhouse with two men holding long guns looking out of a raised window was to the side. The two policemen looked at each other and then looked at the car. Neither showed any expression. One said something to Jose, who got out of the car without turning off the engine. They spoke briefly as the cop opened a pad and pen. It began to rain again, and the sky turned from blue to black. He came around to the driver's side and inspected the backseat and the front while Maria and Lola remained quiet. He closed the pad and threw up his hands.

"*Loco!*" he said to Jose, who got back in as the cop stood up and handed his gun to the man inside the guardhouse.

"*Poncho. Para Mama.*" He yelled.

The man inside handed the poncho to the man outside, who took it and spread it over Maria in the backseat.

"*Mucho gracias,*" Jose said as he pulled away. "*Patria y vida.*"

"*Patria y muerte,*" the man yelled back and grabbed the gun that the other handed him through the window. Jose stopped the car. He came to the passenger side, where Lola sat up.

"*Chicita,*" he demanded. *"Patria y vida o Patria y muerte?"*

"*Rico que Lobo,*" Lola said.

"*Rico que Lobo,*" the cop repeated and laughed, and thunder sent him back to his safe house.

"You are a very smart young woman," Jose said to Lola. They both looked back to see the two policemen leave the guardhouse as

LOLA

the wind toppled it, revealing a car they struggled into and drove off in the other direction.

"Was he going to shoot us?" Lola said.

"No," Jose said. "He wanted to give me a ticket for driving tourists in a storm. I told him it was my wife and daughter and we were going to my father's house. He said the radio advised that the hurricane had changed path and we were heading into it."

"Should we turn around?" Lola asked.

"No." Maria was emphatic from under her cover in the backseat. "We go to family. You go with us. We are your *Familia Cubana, Patria y vida.*"

"What does that mean?" Lola said to Jose, who never took his eyes from the road

"Country and life," he said. "The new revolution. *Patria y muerte,* country and death was the call of the old revolutionaries. They would die for the country. And they would kill for the country, and sadly they did. Cubans killing Cubans. They were not family. They were a band of bandits led by idealists."

"Are you a communist?" Lola said. "I saw pictures of Fidel and Che at your apartment."

"They were revolutionaries," Jose said. "They overthrew a corrupt government of thieves and gangsters. They were fighting for a free Cuba with equality for all. All that talk turned to authoritarianism when they needed money, and the US cut them off. They became communists to please the Russians, who bought all of our sugar and paid to construct bases in Cuba to fight the Americans. After the Americans supported counter-revolutionaries, who invaded Cuba at the Bay of Pigs. That is where we are headed."

"The Bay of Pigs?" Lola questioned.

"*Bahia de Cochinos,*" Jose said. "Or as we Cubans call it the Victory of Giron."

LOLA

"Look out!" Lola shouted as a tree was blown across the highway. "Stop!"

Jose did not hesitate. He stepped on the gas and ran off the highway, turned hard, swinging the rear end around, and powered back onto the highway past the fallen tree with but a few scratches on the passenger side of the car.

"That was close." Lola let out a relaxing breath.

"Never stop for trouble." Jose was calm. "Run away from it. We are the new revolutionaries. We want life for all Cubans. We want to be friends, not enemies. The old guard always needs an enemy to blame for the problems and corruption they have created. Yes, we have good schools. We have good doctors. And for a few extra *cukes*, Cuban pesos, or Euros or dollars, they will even give you an anesthetic."

Jose laughed at his Cuban joke, and Maria chimed in from the backseat.

"*Patria y vida.*"

"If you kill a man," Jose said. "Three years in jail. If you kill a cow, thirty years in jail. Everything for the tourists. Nothing for the *campesinos* but rice, maybe beans, and on a good day a chicken. While the leaders live large."

They were headed out of the cane fields into a jungle of palmetto trees and mangroves. They passed several roadside monuments solid against the swaying trees. The rain had lessened.

Lola watched Jose's face as he kept his eyes on the road and his mind on the revolution to come. "Freedom to speak to travel to learn about the outside world." His eyes widened as he told her about Cuba, its mountains and beaches, fields full of food, and reefs full of marine life. He smiled with pride as he told of a resilient population resourceful enough to survive and dream on a few hundred dollars a month. He had great hopes for the future when the young Cubans took over from the old guard that lived on bribes and graft. He was saddened when they passed the monuments standing solid against the storm

"What are those for?" Lola asked about the markers.

"They are for the fallen defenders who repelled the invasion at Giron sponsored by the US. Cubans killing Cubans. Ours is not a revolution of guns but cellphones. Information, communication, and union. They may have guns, but we have the numbers because all those soldiers and police are people. People with children and families and they all have phones. It may not happen overnight, but over time the young educated men will see a brighter future."
"And women too." Maria would not be left out.

After the mangroves and swamp, they came to a small seaside community with a waterfront resort, a few houses and buildings, a police station, and a dive shop. There was an abandoned produce stand, and more small houses formed a neighborhood. A beach ran along the bay of clear blue water with a dark reef some distance out toward a dark blue sea spotted by whitecaps as the wind increased.

Jose stopped the car in front of a small block house facing the beach. There was no one on the streets. Windows were covered with planks and plastic. There was the clip-clop sound of a horse-drawn carriage full of kids returning from school. They all wore pants or jumpers and white shirts with red ribbons around their necks. Lola could have been one of them.
A covered porch was empty of anything that could blow away. A table could be seen inside the front window propped on end as a shield against the coming storm. A chatter of people could be heard from inside, and the front door opened. A girl about Lola's age ran out

to greet her father and mother with hugs and kisses. Lola watched them, but her mind was far away with another family. Her family.

Lola looked at Jose's daughter Juanita dressed in an orange jumper and white shirt and a blue scarf knotted around her neck. They could have been twins of a different color. Juanita dark, Lola light. Jose introduced them to each other as they rushed into the house. They shook hands and exchanged formal hugs. They both looked at Jose with admiration. They were sisters of a different mother and father but a common instinct for communion.

"BFF," Maria said and held the two girls in her arms.
"BFF," Lola agreed.
"BFF." Juanita laughed at her mother's talk. "There was no electricity at the camp, so we came home in donkey carts."
"OMG," Maria said, and the three of them held tight.
"Girl power!" Juanita said.

It was dark inside the small house that kept the wind and rain out, with the table barricading the front window. The only light came from candles and the orange glow of a cigar burning in the mouth of a drawn-faced old man sitting in a corner chair. The two older women and two small girls attended to him with a glass of rum and a footstool where his scrawny naked feet rested. He didn't get up when Jose bent to kiss him on his wrinkled forehead.

"What have you brought me?" the old man asked as he looked at Lola. "Is this one of my grandchildren? I don't remember any Americana lovers. But maybe. I'm an old man, sometimes I forget. But if her mother looked anything like her, I would remember. You are a very beautiful woman. Come, give this old soldier a kiss. What is your name?"

LOLA

"Lola," she said, and with a nod from Jose, she kissed his father on the unshaven cheek. "And what is your name? You speak English so well."

"They all call me Popo," he said. "I should speak good English. I taught English before I joined the revolution. Fidel was my best student and my best comrade. We were young and full of ambition and goodwill. I was with Fidel on *Grandma*, the boat we lost in our first attempt to overthrow the gangsters that ran the country. We were in jail together, then in the mountains, and finally in Havana. I can tell you stories…"

"Later," Jose said as he peeked around the table, blocking the window and leaning against it to reinforce its protection. "It's getting worse. I can hardly see our neighbor by the market. The market is gone. "

Jose jumped to the side as glass shattered, and a loud bang was heard against the table.

"Cannonballs." Popo reached beside his chair and pulled up a rifle.

"Coconuts," Jose said. "Everyone remain calm. Popo, be careful with that old gun."

"It isn't loaded," Popo said. "I took it from one of the invaders. An M1 supplied by the Americanos at Giron. We showed them. It was a great victory for our small army against the most powerful country. But so many had to die. But not me. I survived and was victorious. Never give up. I can tell you stories…"

He was interrupted by a great wind that rattled the metal roof and shook the stone house to its foundation.

"Everybody to the bedroom." Jose took command and herded the women and children to a smaller room as the table blew down from the broken window onto the floor in front of Popo, who was unmoved. His cigar still burned bright against the storm.

LOLA

"The Russians with their stupid missiles. Such rude people who never tipped. JFK and Krushchev had enough sense not to go to war. Who was the enemy? We needed an enemy to continue our fight. Communists? Capitalists? Cubans." Popo went on unheeded by the storm. "We are now the enemy of the people like my son, the cellphone revolutionary. Where is your revolution when the lights go out?"

Five women and children were on the bed in a room with a small window protected by a sea grape tree that engaged the wind and rain that rattled the glass. Jose stood by the bedroom door, holding it closed against the storm. When there was a pause in the gusts, he opened it slightly to see Popo still sitting in his chair puffing on his cigar.

As the hurricane moved, the wind direction changed from south to west, and the building itself withstood the blasts. It was moving inland. Jose could open the door and see through the broken window to the bay where the clear water was now gray and up over the beach. To the east, he could see what remained of his neighbor's house, the roof was gone, and a woman and two children had tied themselves to the beams that had supported the roof.

Jose gave his phone to Maria to keep it dry. He went out and found a knife in the kitchen, put it in his belt, and returned to the bedroom.

"I have to get them and bring them back." He smiled and gave a hero's salute.

"I'll go with you," Juanita said. "You can't carry all of them. I'm strong."

"I'll go too," Lola said, inspired by her new friend's courage. "We can do this."

LOLA

"If you don't come back," Maria told Jose, holding up his phone, "I will carry on the fight. WTF."

"BFF," Jose and the two girls said together. "Best friends forever!"

The table that had protected them from the broken glass window was again on the floor. The front door had held. Using the upside-down table as a ramp, they carefully went over the sill into a clearing sky and light winds.

"The eye of the storm," Jose said. "It won't last long."

They stepped around the green car full of water that was slowly draining through holes in the old floorboards. A blue sky ringed in a circle of black clouds that flashed with lightning. Thunder rumbled everywhere in the distance. Their destination was past where the produce stand had been. The ground was covered with water, broken fronds and debris, grasses, shells, and unknowns from the shore.

"Keep behind me," Jose said as he navigated a path toward the woman and children still hanging in the rafters. It was slow going with gusts pushing them then opposing them. They marched with their heads down, and eyes squinted. Only Jose looked up to see the closing hurricane eye and out to the bay to see the rising water covering their ankles. Juanita held on to Jose's shirttail, and Lola held one of the straps to Juanita's jumper. Two students on a field trip with their instructor.

At the house, the rafters were too high for Jose to reach with his knife.

"I can hold up both of you," he said. "One on each shoulder. Juanita, take the knife. Lola, catch the babies. I'll get the woman when she falls. Tell her to hold on until you two get the children down."

Jose stooped down so the two schoolgirls could mount his broad shoulders. He stood up. Juanita was short of her goal. She looked at Lola in her squinted eyes.

LOLA

"I have to stand up," Juanita said. "I can do it. I practice gymnastics. Just hold my legs."

Juanita had lost her shoes in the trek and was barefoot with the knife in her teeth as she used Jose's head for balance to go straight up to the beams.

Lola still wore her rope sandals. Lola wrapped her arms around Juanita's legs as she sawed through the ropes until one child was free and dropped down to Lola, who caught her with one arm while the other held tight to Juanita's legs.

The second child was unbound and fell onto Juanita's chest, and then she slid down one side of Jose while Lola carried the baby down the other side.

The woman praised God and let go of the beam clutching at Jose as she hit the water, and he caught her and laughed out loud as a rebuke to the storm that closed the eye and brought water up to their knees. Lola steadied him by leaning against his back as he maneuvered the woman who had a large belly so that she rested cradled in his arms.

The walk back to their house was easier now, with the water pushing them as it rose. They handed their treasures through the front window to Maria and the other woman who took them into the bedroom. The front door and stone walls had held, and Popo still smoked his cigar in his chair.

"This house is my reward from the party for killing Cubans at Giron," Popo said. "Sixty years ago. Nobody today remembers yesterday. We were so young and brave and full of ourselves. Look at me now. Jose, my son. Look at the future of the revolutionary. *Patria y muerte. Muerte*, death. Sooner or later. Always death."

"*Patria y vida*," Jose responded. "You're not dead yet. Come into the bedroom."

LOLA

"A warrior dies on the battlefield, not in the bedroom." Popo laughed. "This house and I will be here when the storm is gone."

Maria and the girls exchanged a high five.
"Girl power!"

In the bedroom, there were three women, four children, and two girls on the bed. The children clung to their mothers in the middle while Maria and the girls sat on the edges with their feet up out of the water. Lola took off her sandals and tied them to her jumper straps with the scarf she had worn around her neck. Jose stood in the water and closed the bedroom door behind him as he went back into the living room when he saw the waterfall over the front window sill filling the house.

Jose saw the glow of Popo's cigar disappear before he could reach him. Popo sank beneath the flow, never leaving his chair, his eyes defiant before they closed. Jose tried to pull him up but was washed aside as the front door gave in against the flood, and the entire house was moved with its foundation back into the mangroves at the edge of the swamp.

Water could be seen outside the bedroom window when the tree protecting it disappeared, but the glass still held, and they felt themselves moving in the stone house that held together then shuddered as it hit the mangroves and stopped. The women all said prayers and held their children closer. The two girls held each other. Lola calmed herself by controlling her breath, and the calm passed to Juanita. They were brave.

"Jose!" Maria called.

The bedroom door was closed with water now on both sides, reaching the bottom of the mattress. It was as if the house had exhaled when the roof came off and crashed into the swamp. They could see the dark sky and feel the rapid-fire of rain against their faces as they looked up for heaven but soon bowed their heads and endured the fury of nature's wrath. They were alive. The roar of the wind overwhelmed their senses and thoughts. There was no concept of time. There was only the present. Keep the children alive even though their cries could not be heard. Only God could hear their prayers.

"Jose!" Maria called again as the wind died down and the rain fell in droplets rather than darts.

The flood had peaked but still filled the room. Daylight was leaving them. It would soon be night.

Lola could feel her hands shaking, and she released Juanita, who moved to her mother's side and held on like the other children. Lola had no one to go to for comfort. She was alone in a crowd. She was alive. She breathed in hope and exhaled fear. She was alive. The room and the world became quiet.

"*Mi agua!*" the round woman cried. "*Mi agua!*"

"She wants water," Juanita said.

"No, no," Maria said as she saw the wetness spread from between the woman's legs as she lay on her back. "Her water broke. Take the children."

"She's having a baby," Juanita told Lola, and they picked up the two young children they had rescued and stood in the water while the other woman with her two children did the same.

"Give her something to bite on," Maria said when the woman screamed. She pointed to the rope sandals around Lola's jumper. Lola untied the one with the ankle strap and gave it to her. Another scream! Maria placed the strap in the woman's mouth. She knew what she was doing. The scream was replaced by the increasing buzz of mosquitos that descended upon them when the wind disappeared.

There was no way to avoid the stings as everybody had their hands full, unable to even swat at the new enemy. It was getting darker outside. The woman moaned.

"I need some light," Maria said.

Lola handed her the child and searched the pockets of her jumper until she found her cellphone. It had a light. It worked. Lola shined it between the woman's legs. A round hairy ball covered with blood was stuck there.

"Push, push," Juanita echoed her mother's directions for Lola, who held the light steady. *"Empujar! Empujar!"*

The other woman joined in, *"Empujar! Empujar!"*

Then all of them, including the children who could talk, joined the choir as they slapped at the enemy.

"Empujar! Empujar. Push, push!" They spoke the English they had learned in school.

The round head with black hair mixed with blood came out, and its mouth opened for its first breath. It slid into Maria's hands, followed by the bloody afterbirth and umbilical. Maria lifted the baby by its feet and smacked him on his bottom to clear his lungs.

"Muchacho!" Maria said and took the rope sandal from the mother's mouth.

The mother let out an endless sigh and cried tears of joy, and everyone cheered.

"It's a boy," Juanita told Lola, who shone her light on the baby while Maria bit through the umbilical cord and knotted the piece next to the boy's genitals. Maria wiped the baby's face with her dress and placed him on his mother's naked breast. Lola saw his eyes open. He let out a cry.

LOLA

"He's alive!" Lola said as the phone light faded into the night. They all had seen the miracle.
Life.

LOLA

PART FIVE

The sea moved back into the bay, leaving behind a coating of white sand everywhere it had been. The clouds parted, revealing the full moon that had inspired the flood. The white sand and the water in the bay reflected silver. It was easy for the people in the stone house to see the aftermath.

From their new location further back against the mangroves, they could see a panorama of damage, fallen trees, destroyed buildings, and assorted seagrass and shells. Up the beach stood a house seemingly untouched by the storm showing the selective nature of wind and water. The house belonged to the woman with two children who had chosen to seek safety in the stone house relocated with its rock foundation and the earthen rise on which it was built. The green car was still where Jose had parked it at the bottom of the rise. Beyond it was a wide view of the beach since the state-owned resort had disappeared.

The beach was empty but twice as far away as it had been. The waters of the bay were calm. A ship had been grounded on the sandbank, but a passing cloud shadow made it difficult to see it completely.

"I'll take care of everything here," Maria said. "Juanita, take Lola out and look for Jose. I'm sure he found a safe place. He is a strong swimmer. Look on the beach."

Lola put on her rope sandals and held Juanita's hand as they went out into the main house. The water was gone. Popo was still there.

LOLA

Popo was seated in his chair with his eyes closed. He was dusted with sand and wet to the bone of his thin body. Juanita went to him and brushed sand from the few white hairs on his head, and kissed him goodbye. Under the sand, his face was gray and smoothly relaxed. His rifle was still in his lap.

"*Te amo,*" Juanita said. "I love you."

She started to laugh and urged Lola to come see. She pointed to Popo's mouth. Clenched in his teeth was the butt of a cigar.

"He never surrendered." Maria came out to see. "He was a good man. He only cared about the Cuban people. "

From deep inside the chair wedged behind the pillow for his back was a box of cigars. Maria took one out and lit it. She filled the air with smoke.

"This will help keep the enemy away," she said. "Mosquitos are the enemy, Popo."

Maria managed to pry the butt from between his teeth and replaced it with the cigar she had lit. It smoldered there. She put her arm around Juanita's shoulder.

"Never give up," she told the girls. "Now go and find Jose."

The girls walked out where the front door had been onto a slope of soft sand that led down to the green convertible with the top still held to the frame by a strand. It had filled with water that now drained slowly through the floorboards, revealing what was left wedged under the front seat where Lola had been. It was her big brother's blue shirt. It was too wet to wear, but she wrapped it around her waist without hesitation as she was also wet.

She saw Juanita swat at her face. Lola unwrapped the shirt and shared it with Juanita. They each put a naked arm into an empty sleeve and covered their faces with the tails against their enemy.

LOLA

They walked together like conjoined twins, carefully stepping over debris and uprooted seagrass, looking at the ground as they made their way to the beach. They were blessed with a breeze off the bay that was their ally against the enemy mosquitos. The shirt came off, and their clothes started to dry. They were able to see the beach and the bay. The boat on the sandbank had lights on. It was too far away to see any activity.

They were now on the beach approaching the shoreline. There was something at the water's edge. What was it? A palm log?

A body!

Juanita's scream was so loud it could be heard back at the stone house. It shook Lola to her heart. She saw the profile of Jose against the white sand. Her heart dropped into the deep black eye of the shark and fell to hell. They were both frozen until the shore break moved over the body and turned it on its side, and they could see water spill from his mouth.

As one the two girls ran to Jose without speaking, their throats choked up but their minds alert. He was naked but for a pair of brief underwear like the ones Lola's big brother wore. He was covered with sand that Juanita had to brush away from his mouth when they turned him onto his back and began to go to work.

Lola was on her knees beside him feeling his stomach for where his ribs began. A hand's width to his breast bone. She made her hands into a pump and began compressions. Juanita tilted his head back, pinched his nose shut, lifted his chin, and blew three quick breaths.

"One, two, three, four, five..." Lola counted out loud to fifteen.
Breath.
"One, two, three, four, five...fifteen."
Breath.
"One, two, three, four, five...fifteen."

79

LOLA

Breath.

They were in a rhythmic zone. There was no future. There was no past. They were on autopilot. They moved with the pulse of the universe.

"One, two, three, four, five..."

Breath.

Maria had run down from the house at the sound of Juanita's scream. She fell to her knees at Jose's feet. She prayed.

"One, two, three, four, five..."

Breath.

"Lover, companion, comrade," Maria said to Jose. "Please don't leave me now."

"One, two, three, four, five..."

Breath.

"You have strong hands," Maria said to Lola. "But I believe he is in the hands of God."

"Never give up," Juanita answered.

Lola continued her compressions.

"One, two, three, four, five...fifteen."

Breath.

Juanita cried quietly as she continued to breathe into her father. Tears ran down her face and fell into his open mouth.

Jose coughed.

Lola collapsed onto Jose's chest. Her head was turned to the side with her ear against his breast bone. She heard it.

A heartbeat.

One, two, three, four, five...

LOLA

Maria moved around to turn Jose onto his side. Jose coughed again, and the sea came up from inside and spilled water, grass, sand, and shells onto the ground. He coughed and breathed.

"Massage," a voice said. "His arms, his legs, his back. Squeeze his calves, his second heart. The calf muscles pump as much blood as his heart."

Lola followed the instructions from an accented voice. She looked up and saw a white-haired angel in white clothes holding a flashlight and a black bag. The angel stood over them and took a small bottle from the bag. She poured an amber liquid into Jose's mouth, and he coughed again and gasped a large breath of air. There was a strong smell of alcohol as he exhaled.

"Cognac," the angel said and then gave herself a taste.

Juanita brushed sand from Jose's eyes, and they opened. Lola and Maria continued the massage. The angel took another sip.
"Am I alive?" Jose asked the angel in white that stood over him.
"Lazarus phenomenon." Her accent was French.
"Where did you come from?" Lola asked.
"Heaven sent," Maria said.
"Perhaps," the angel said. "My name is Simone. My ship is aground on the seagrass. We are making a movie for *National Geographic*. That's not important now. We have to get this man up after a few minutes to see if the magic works."
All four women worked on Jose. One on each arm and each leg. He blinked his eyes and moved his fingers and toes as the circulation returned.

"I saw you from my boat with binoculars," Simone said. "You girls were miraculous. I could use one of you in my movie.

LOLA

PART SIX

"Where did you girls learn to do CPR?" Simone asked.

"Swim team," Lola said, continuing the massage.

"YouTube," Juanita said.

"Maria," Jose said softly. "I love you."
"Compadre," Maria said to him and kissed the leg she was rubbing.

They continued to rub until Jose began to move.
"Are you okay?" Simone asked.
"I don't know," Jose said.
"What happened?" Maria asked.
"Nothing," Jose whispered. "There is a hole in my life."

"You were dead for a while," Simone said. "Then like Lazarus, you returned,"
Then to the women. "It is not unheard of. There are documented cases. Google it. Lazarus phenomenon."
"How do you know so much?" Lola asked.
"I've been on boats since I was younger than you girls," Simone said. "Many sailors have died at sea. This is not my first miracle. Let's

try to get him up before the tide comes in, and I have to get back to my boat."

Maria and Simone helped Jose sit up, and he coughed and coughed. They stopped to let him recover. Then one woman under each arm and the girls standing front and back raised him to his feet, and all four steadied him until he regained his balance.

"One step at a time," Simone cautioned. "One step at a time."

Jose took his first deep breath and exhaled slowly. He didn't cough. He smiled.

"I'm going home," Jose said and looked away from the water to where he thought the stone house should be.

Lola looked at him and wished that she could say the same thing. She found her big brother's blue shirt on the sand. It was wet, but she draped it over her shoulders.

With her flashlight, Simone found the pattern of Lola's rope sandals on a path away from the beach. She wore white canvas shoes and stepped into the footprints one step at a time. They were on their way.

One step at a time.

Clouds passed over the moon from time to time, but they continued rhythmically. One step at a time. It was difficult to see the house against the broken pattern of the mangroves. Where the house should have been, they saw an empty spot when the moon came back out. There was a distant flash of light far away in the darkness.

"Headlights!" Maria said. "Help has arrived."

LOLA

The closer they got to the house, they could see many lights moving along the road through the mangroves. They could even hear voices shouting orders as they reached the green car. They were halfway home. One step at a time.

Jose wanted to stop at the car. He tried to speak, but his voice was frozen. He managed to touch Maria's face. She understood what he wanted. Their minds were the same as their souls.

They all stopped and breathed deeply as Jose touched the trunk of the car. He drew strength from his chariot. It also had a soul. The spirit in the sand he walked on energized his bare feet. Jose became strong. He still held on to the women who gave him his greatest strength.

"I am alive," Jose said when they came close enough to see the stone house clearly in the moonlight.

There was a lot of activity. A generator could be heard. There were lights. The shadows of many people could be seen. Motors and voices mixed in the background. All converged in the stone house.

"Popo es muerte," a woman's voice from the house said to a man who stood outside directing the activity inside.

The man directed other men to be careful as they moved Popo from his chair. The glow of the cigar in his mouth burned bright when a long ash fell from it onto his naked chest. The gun in his lap never moved.

Jose let out a laugh as they were now close enough to see Popo lifted from his chair, cigar in mouth and gun in hand.

Never give up.

"Who goes there?" a man demanded.
"Patria y muerte," Jose said. "Never give up. "
"Patria y vida," Lola said.

LOLA

"*Langostina!*" the man in charge said when he turned around and saw her with Jose and the other women. "The police at the checkpoint reported seeing you. I was sent to take you back. They just want to ask you a few questions."

"You are mistaken," Juanita said. "This is my sister."

"Lola Lobo," Diego said. "You will not fool me again. I talked to El Capitano before taking his boat out ahead of the storm. He didn't want to be blown up on the dock and lose his ship. Foolish man. The Coast Guard reported a capsized fishing boat halfway to Key West."

"And the crew?" Lola said.

"No bodies were found," Diego said.

"*Senor,*" Simone interrupted, "my boat is on the sandbank. Is there a boat available to help me out?"

Diego was distracted by the woman in white.

"How are the babies in the house?" Maria said.

"The doctor said they are fine," Diego said, referring to the woman who had pronounced Popo dead. "We have no tugboats," he said to Simone. "Where are your papers?"

"On the boat," Simone replied. "I will go get them."

"Be careful with Popo," Jose yelled, his voice and strength having returned. "He was a hero in the battle of Giron. The state will want to put up a memorial for him like the others on the highway."

"Be careful," Diego warned the men in green uniforms who were handling the body. "He is a hero."

"Come sit down now and rest," Maria said to Jose and moved him into his father's chair with her and Juanita standing at his sides

"*Patria y vida,*" Jose said. "Please get me a cigar."

Lola looked at Jose, Maria, and Juanita. They were her *Familia Cubana.* She felt someone touch her arm. It was Simone.

"I just want to get back to my family," Lola said, feeling the blue shirt she wore.

85

LOLA

"Come with me," Simone said. "I can get you home."

They snuck away like thieves in the night. Lola walked in front in her rope sandals. In her white canvas shoes, Simone walked behind, hiding Lola from anyone looking from the house. They were silent until they reached the green car near where the stone house had once been. It had been an ordinary house with flowers and plants on the porch. Now it was an empty space but for a few overturned pots half-buried in the sand. Lola stopped suddenly, and Simone almost walked into her with a questioning look at the girl.

"Aloe," Lola whispered.

She stooped down and uncovered a clay pot to find her treasure. It was the spiked green leaves of the succulent. Lola used her big brother's blue shirt to protect her hands as she pulled the plant from the pot. She then continued on her path to the beach, where she could see Simone's rubber dinghy anchored near the waterline.

It was a gray inflatable with a hard wooden floor where a pair of oars had been stowed under a red plastic seat inserted in both sides across the width of the boat. Simone lifted the anchor from the sand that held it to the land and placed it in the boat's bow, which she pushed into deeper water. She then swung herself over the side onto the seat and picked up the oars. She placed them in oarlocks and maneuvered the boat sideways so Lola could pull herself aboard into the bow, where she slunk down, careful not to sit on the anchor while hiding from the view from the house. The aloe plant pricked her through the shirt, but she didn't mind. She was safe.

Simone rowed quietly until they were far enough out of hearing range of anyone who might have followed them. She rested and floated. Over her shoulder, she could see her ship resting motionless on the sandbank. It was farther away than it looked, rowing against the wind and the incoming tide. She dipped the oars and resumed her stroke. She took a deep breath of relief and relaxation, her rowing motion as natural as the rhythm of the sea.

"Are you in trouble?" Simone asked Lola.

"It's a long story," Lola said.

"We have time," Simone said. "It's a long ride."

"It all started when I fell off of the cruise ship." Lola began leaning closer so Simone could hear. She continued. "I was saved from a shark by some dolphins. Then I was picked up by some pirates, El Capitano, Paulie, and Manuel the long-haired motherfucker."

Simone listened without losing a stroke.

"They brought me to Cuba," Lola went on. "They warned me that since I didn't have any papers, I would probably wind up in a Cuban jail. So they gave me to Jose to help me out. We wound up at Popo's house, where I watched a baby born in the middle of the storm. When the storm was over, we found Jose on the beach. You know the rest."

"Did you leave anything out?" Simone said. "Why did that policeman want you?"

"He's just doing his job," Lola said.

"A policeman is a policeman everywhere in the world." Simone smiled. "Eric Maria Remarque wrote that."

"The policeman is also involved in the drug smuggling and money smuggling commerce," Lola said.

Simone laughed out loud.

LOLA

"That's quite a story," Simone said. "Who are you, and what do you want?"

"I am who I am, and I just want to be happy," Lola said without too much thought.

Simone laughed again.

"What a wonderful girl you are," Simone said.

They could hear voices from the ship as they approached. Someone spotted them and came to the bow and threw a line to them. Simone caught it and pulled them alongside. While Simone tied the dinghy to the ship, a shirtless man extended a ladder over the side for Lola to climb. She handed her aloe plant up to him.

Lola remembered the climb up the cruise ship ladder. It had been painful to her hands and feet. This ladder was a pleasure. It had wooden steps instead of metal rungs. The sides were rounded wood and did not cut into her hands.

Before she started up, she took off her rope sandals. She tied them to the sleeve of her shirt. They had sentimental value too.

The ship was bigger than the fishing boat by twice the size as far as she could see. It was well out of the water, which wasn't deep. As she took the first step, she looked to the rear where Simone had tied off the dinghy. Halfway up, Lola stopped to watch as Simone pulled herself up on a line that anchored the stern, then swung herself over the back onto the boat.

"Awesome!"

Lola continued her climb until she reached the top and was helped onboard by a shirtless man in a Speedo and a topless girl in a sarong. Simone had reached them quickly. They all paid little attention to Lola.

"Good news, bad news, Mo?" Simone said to the man.

LOLA

"Good news," Mo said. "We aren't going to sink. Bad news. Because we are already on the bottom."

"Any damage to the hull?" Simone asked.

"A hole port side forward of the engine room. Gus and Richard are assessing the situation. I think we landed on the only coral on this entire grassy sandbank."

"Let me take a look," Simone said to him and then to the topless girl, "Arleen, take Lola to my cabin and get her cleaned up and fed. I'm sure you must have some clothes that she can wear. Throw her uniform into the laundry with her socks."

Simone yelled back as she left with Mo, "And get her a tampon."

"How did she know?" Lola said.

"She knows everything," Arleen said. "Maybe it's the red streak running down your white socks. "

"OMG!" Lola said. "I forgot about that."

"WTF," Arleen said. "Follow me, and don't worry if you drip on the deck. I'll clean it up. That's my job."

The deck was wide and long like a barge. At the bow, which faced the beach, there was a large winch with a chain around it. As they walked toward the stern, they passed in front of the control tower and bridge, which rose high enough to see the entire deck. Behind that wheelhouse was more deck and a high transom. They entered a door below the bridge to a stairway that led up and down. They came to a heavy teak door one level below. It opened into a large comfortable room with a king-size bed and a table to one side. Above the table, there were several computer screens and darkened instrument panels. A bathroom with an open shower and toilet was next to one side of the bed. Above the bed was a large hatch big enough to climb through. The hum of a generator could be felt if not heard.

LOLA

"Don't worry about water," Arleen told Lola as she escorted her to the shower. "Do what you have to do. That storm filled up all our reserve water tanks with fresh water. Leave your clothes on the floor. I'll get them when I come back. There are fresh towels above the toilet that you can flush with the red button on the handle."

"Thank you very much, " Lola said.

"All part of my job," Arleen said and went out of the room.

Lola looked around at the polished teak trim and shiny brass fixtures. She felt as if she had fallen into a luxury suite. She looked at the bed neatly made with a colorful spread. The bed beckoned to her exhausted body as she undressed and found the controls for the shower. The hot water was just hot enough, and the cold was refreshing. There was shampoo and soap in small plastic bottles stored above a basin in the shower stall.

Lola rubbed the shampoo into her hair and inhaled the scent of lavender. The bubbles ran down her body to her feet that were white from being too long in the sea. With the soap and a washcloth, she cleaned the creases in her body. A pump kicked in as the water drained through the floor.

Lola wrapped a towel around her as she stepped out into the room. There was no one there, so she quickly dried her hair as not to drip on anything. She saw that her dirty clothes had been picked up and her phone was on a charger by the instrument panels. A pair of white cotton underpants and a small white bag with toilet paper and a tampon were on the bed. There was a large T-shirt with a picture of Che on the front.

Lola went back into the shower and put her used tampon in the bag wrapped in toilet paper. She noticed that the bleeding was light. She dressed in the T-shirt and pants. She heard someone on the steps.

90

LOLA

Arleen came in with a tray of tea, two cups, and croissants. Lola's aloe plant was sitting by the door. The tray was set on the table by the panels.

"Thank you so much," Lola said.

"You're welcome," Arleen said. "Is there anything else you need?"

"I'm not quite sure," Lola said. "My mind hasn't caught up with my body."

"Just rest," Arleen said. "If you're awake before breakfast, we can do yoga on deck with the sunrise."

"Wonderful," Lola said. "You have an awesome body. Do you always go topless?"

"Sometimes I take off the bottom too. I haven't had any complaints." Arleen smiled and unwrapped the sarong enough to flash her toned abs and unshaved lower parts. She rewrapped and sat on the edge of the bed while Lola went for the tea and food.

"I can't remember the last time I ate," Lola said.

"This is a clothing-optional crew," Arleen said. "Don't be surprised by the naked men. After a while, you get used to it. It's more comfortable in this climate, and no one gets excited. "

"I understand," Lola said, slowly eating and drinking as she sat in a chair pulled out from beneath the table. "This is some boat, and this cabin is like something out of an old pirate movie."

"Captain Blood," Arleen said. "Rich designed it. He's somewhat a romantic. You'll meet him later, but right now, he's down in the bilge taking care of his investment. He built this boat for Simone. "

"What is Captain Blood, Alex?" Lola said.

"Alex?" Arleen said.

"It's a game show on television, *Jeopardy*," Lola said.

"I don't watch television," Arleen said. "Rich put a cellular one on the boat for the crew."

"It must have cost a fortune," Lola said.

LOLA

"He has a fortune," Arleen said.

There were footsteps on the stairs. Simone came in looking worried but smiled when she saw the two girls. Without saying a word, she went directly to the shower. She stripped off her white clothes and canvas shoes and left them on the floor.

Arleen got up and took the laundry with her as she left the cabin. She dropped the clothes outside and came back into the desk by the panel. She opened a lower drawer, took out a silver flask, and put it next to the empty cup on the tray.

"Your job," Lola said.

"I'm lucky to have a job." Arleen blew a kiss to Lola as she went out the door, closing it behind her.

"What a treasure," Simone said as she went to the tray. "That girl is a free spirit and reads peoples' minds. She knows what somebody wants before they know they want it."

Simone poured an amber shot into the cup and downed it with a gratified sigh. She was completely naked. Her body was lean with defined muscles under loose skin. The hair between her legs and under her arms matched the short white hair on her head. She was tan as teak except for the soles of her feet that were the waterlogged white that Lola was familiar with as her feet were the same.

"I'm so glad you brought that aloe," Simone said. "I see you've picked up some local knowledge. Be a dear, and please rub some of that on our feet. Come here next to me on the bed. I get the side closest to the head, the bathroom, and you get my husband Philippe's side. You should fit right into the impression he leaves when he's not here. He should be back tomorrow."

92

LOLA

Lola broke off one of the leaves of the aloe. She used her thumbnail to split it down the middle the way she remembered from the lobster boat. That seemed like ages ago. Simone turned on her side and bent her legs so her feet were where Lola could reach them. Lola tore the aloe in half and used one side for Simone, drifting away. She used the other half on herself.

"Gus will take care of everything," Simone said. "If there is a problem he can't solve, I'll be the first to know. *Dorme bien.* Sweet dreams. You have healing hands, *Langostina.*"

Lola finished her tea. It tasted like chamomile. Then she ate the other croissant. She didn't want it to go bad. She looked at her phone, changed her mind, and was asleep as soon as her head felt the pillow.

LOLA

PART SEVEN

Lola and Simone awoke at the same time to the smell of coffee before the sun was up. A tray had been placed on the desk with two cups. One had a tea bag string draped over the rim. The other had a spoon sticking out.

"Good morning," Arleen said as she came in with a stack of folded clothes that she placed at the foot of the bed.

"Thank you," Simone said and unwrapped herself from the sheet that covered her. She stretched and yawned.

"Jasmine tea for you," Arleen told Lola and set the tray between the two women in bed. "Then yoga on the bow before breakfast."

"Jasmine. How did you know?" Lola asked her.

Arleen just smiled and went to the bottom drawer of the desk and took out the silver flask. She handed it to Simone, who took a swig and handed it back, and it was replaced in the drawer. Arleen blew them both a kiss and, with a namaste, bowed and left the room.

Lola sipped her tea and looked at the stack of clothes. She saw the school uniform she had borrowed from Juanita with the shirt and socks. She touched them.

"I have to return these," Lola told Simone.

"No problem," Simone said and drank her coffee. "I plan to go in again to check on Jose while you and Arleen do your yoga. I'll be back in time for breakfast with the crew."

LOLA

"I'd like to call my mother," Lola said. "Do you have WiFi?"

"Rich has his own satellite," Simone got up and retrieved Lola's phone. "Let me put in the password. Awesome! When did you take this?"

Simone handed the phone to Lola that showed the selfie with the dolphins.

"Just before El Capitano picked me up," Lola said.

Simone took back the phone, pushed a few buttons, and then gave the phone to Lola.

"I'll ask about El Capitano and his crew," Simone said. "You see that hatch behind the bed. That's the escape hatch. Never sleep in a bunk without a hatch big enough to crawl through."

The clear hatch showed that it was still dark outside.

"And always be able to pull yourself on board," Simone advised. "When I can no longer do that, I'll stop sailing."

"I saw you crawl up the anchor line," Lola said. "That was awesome."

"For someone my age?" Simone said. She put on her clean white clothes. She opened the escape hatch to cool air. She climbed through and was gone.

Lola put on the clean panties and the clean faded blue shirt. Buttons were missing, and the collar was ripped. She took a deep breath and smiled. She punched in the numbers for FaceTime on her mother's phone. It was early, but she knew she slept with her phone. She was always prepared for emergencies.

"It's Lola!" Lola's mother yelled loud enough to wake everybody in the house. "You're alive!"

"And well," Lola added. "I'm on a dive boat off of Cuba. They're doing a movie for *National Geographic,* and I'm going to be in it."

LOLA

"Slow down," her mom said. "What happened to the other boat and your friend Manuel the long-haired?"

"That boat capsized in the hurricane." Lola held back tears, and her throat got tight.

Lola saw her father's sleepy-eyed face move next to her mother. He was speechless but happy. Her parents kissed as if to celebrate.

Lola's big brother showed up in the back of them with a smile on his face that Lola recognized. It was the way he looked when he won an argument and was right. She knew he had told her parents that she would be alright while they worried.

"What have you done with my shirt?" he asked.

"You won't believe it when I tell you." Lola laughed.

"What's the name of the boat you're on?" her father asked.

"The *Bob Marley*," Arleen said as she came in behind Lola.

"And what is your name?" Her big brother smiled and asked the tall topless blonde.

"Arleen," she said and returned his smile.

"Can I have your contact information?" he said.

"I don't have a cellphone," Arleen said. "But I know how to use one. I'm sure Lola has your number on her phone. Right now, we have to do our yoga before the crew gets up and wants me to make breakfast. I'm the help."

"I'll send you a long text later," Lola said. "I'm good. How are all of you?"

"Much better now," her mother said.

"I'll make sure she calls back later," Arleen said. "After we fix the hole in the bottom of the boat."

"Don't worry," Lola said. "It's all good. Love you. Over and out."

LOLA

Lola and Arleen exited the same hatch Simone had used to get to the stern. The *Bob Marley* was facing the beach. North. They walked barefoot in silence as they made their way to the bow along the wooden deck. They went past four open hatches that marked the staterooms where the crew slept. There was much more deck before they got to the big winch that held the anchor chain. The boat was huge.

Together the two girls began their yoga in silence. They were side by side but safely apart. They moved in unison without looking at each other. Their minds and bodies were connected, as were their souls. They were soul sisters.

Sun salutation, down dog, up dog, warrior, etcetera until they lay in corpse pose looking up at the lingering stars with the moon gone and a sliver of light on the eastern horizon. They meditated and listened to the sounds of the sea, the wind and moans, and groans coming from the open hatches.

There was a female sigh of satisfaction and loud laughter.

"That's Franco and Lawanda," Arleen said. "Next, you will hear Mo reciting his morning prayers. Then Gus will roar to let them all know it is time to begin work. "

"What about the other cabin?" Lola asked.

"That's Rich's cabin," Arleen said. "He's kind of quiet. But I'm sure he slept down below protecting his investment, making sure the bilge pumps kept working."

There was another loud sigh of satisfaction from Lawanda.

"Do you have a boyfriend?" Arleen asked Lola.

"No," Lola said, "but I did meet this guy on the cruise ship, and we had a mutual attraction. He kissed me."

"You're a virgin?" Arleen said.

"Yes," Lola said matter of factly.

LOLA

"That's good," Arleen said. "I ran away from home when I was fourteen because I wasn't a virgin. I live life as it is, not as it was or will be."

"Amen," Lola said, and they both laughed as the sun brightened the horizon.

They stood up together, faced each other, did a namaste, and bowed. They could hear the splash of oars as Simone rowed back to the stern. They could see her as she pulled herself aboard. Then the lights came on in the control room. It was another day in paradise, but somebody had to do it.

"Time to meet the crew," Arleen said.

Lola's mouth dropped open when she saw two sections in the center of the deck open up like a draw bridge. There were solar panels on the inside surfaces. When the sections were erect, they turned to face the rising sun. Below inside was a large salon with a long table under the portholes on one side. Across from that was a fully equipped galley.

"Rich's idea," Arleen said. "The whole boat is electric, even the engines. And we do have a diesel generator for backup. Look down there. They're coming out of their cabins. The tall shirtless dark one with the knitted skull cap and speedo is Mo. Mohammed. He's Egyptian and one of the world's best freedivers from the Red Sea."

Mo sat at the table that had been set with plates, utensils, coffee, juices, and croissants. He looked up at the two girls on the mahogany stairs that led below. He bowed and showed prayer hands.

"*Langostina*," Mo yelled. "Welcome aboard. As-salumu alaykum."

LOLA

"How did you know that name?" Lola said.

A man and a woman were the next to arrive. She was a black woman with a buzzcut. He was slender, deeply tanned, full head of black hair and a clean-shaven face. They wore matching blue tank tops with Calypso insignias, brief bottoms, and no shoes.

"Lawanda and Franco," Arleen told Lola.

"We know all about you and your story, Lola Lobo," Lawanda said. "Simone told Gus, and Gus told everyone else. You look like a size two."

"You've been shanghaied," Franco said. "We also saw your selfie with the dolphins. I guess Simone wanted us to see that you are right for the part."

"What part?" Lola asked.

"The Silver Bullet," Franco said.

"That's the dive suit I wore for the movie before I started to show." Lawanda lifted her shirt and patted her bare belly in the middle of her black bikini. "It's all Franco's fault. He can't control himself."

"Who can't control himself?" Franco was defensive. "I only wanted to make you happy. "

"I'm very happy, Uncle Frank." Lawanda leaned into him with a gentle kiss.

"That's what she calls him when she's happy," Arleen said and went to the galley to prepare breakfast. "She sounded very happy this morning."

"Sit down and eat. It's going to be a long day," Franco said, drinking his coffee from a bowl. He poured some orange juice for Lawanda. She thanked him in French.

"Uncle Frank was the nicest person in my family," Lawanda said. "All the rest were shits. I swore that if I ever met a man as nice as he was, I'd marry him. Then I met Franco, and now I don't fit into the silver bullet. Every morning now, he whispers, 'Let's tap Tommy on the head.' You know what that means?"

"We heard all about it this morning," Arleen said. She came over with a plate of hot pancakes. "Carbo stacking."

"Size two," Franco said. "We can match it with the footage we got with Lawanda. The silver bullet has a hood and gloves. Your face will be covered with a mask. I'll shoot it, so your eyes never show. It will be perfect."

"Inshallah," Mo said. "Where I come from, we say 'Man plans, God laughs.'"

Simone came into the dining hall.

"Has everyone met," she said and grabbed a cup and a pancake that she ate by hand. "I'm going below to relieve Gus and Rich. They'll fill you in on our plan."

Mo laughed until he caught a glare from the captain. Simone leaned in close to talk to Lola. It was personal but not private.

"I saw Diego," Simone said. "El Capitano and Paulie were pulled up by a helicopter. There was no sign of Manuel the long-haired motherfucker. But they haven't searched the boat yet. They will send divers."

"He'll be alright," Arleen said.

"Inshallah," Mo said.

Simone left for the bilge after grabbing a second pancake and more coffee. The crew sat quietly until she was gone continuing to carbo stack. Then Lawanda had to speak up.

"She's a crazy old lady," Lawanda said.

"Stop," Franco said.

"No," Lawanda said. "We all know. Lola should know too."

LOLA

"I agree," Mo said. "You slept with her last night. Did she tell you about Philippe?"

"She said he would be back today," Lola said.

"Philippe is not coming today," Lawanda said. "Philippe is dead."

"It has nothing to do with our job," Franco said. "She tells everyone he's coming tomorrow."

"She likes to have someone lay down next to her until she falls asleep," Mo said. "We talk about her Jewish family that escaped to France to avoid Auschwitz, and I tell her about my cousins in Gaza. We talk about my family. Then in the middle of a sentence, she is out like a light."

"She has a way to get to your core," Arleen said and set a large pitcher of protein shakedown for everyone to take as they pleased. "I told her about my two abortions. One from rape. One from incest."

Lola and Lawanda both stopped eating and reached a hand out to her.

"Life is what is, not what was or will be," Lola quoted Arleen.

"Amen," Arleen said. Her eyes looked moist, but she laughed. "You're a very fast learner, Lola Lobo."

"When I was with her," Lawanda said. "She told me that Philippe had just left. I humored her. But when I laid down in the impression he left it was warm."

Gus came into the room. He was a large man with a full beard and brown hair to match. He wiped his sweaty forehead with a napkin by one of the plates that Arleen filled with pancakes. He wore a too-short black and white kaftan.

"I heard we had a guest," Gus said, "so I decided to dress for the occasion."

LOLA

"Rich will be out as soon as he showers. He'll fill you all in on the details."

"Was he up all night with the bilge pump?" Mo asked.

"He's one hell of a man," Gus said. "Especially for someone his age."

"And his money," Lawanda said. "If he starts looking for his glasses, don't tell him they're on top of his head."

They all laughed, except clueless Lola, as it was an inside joke.

Rich came in with a big smile on his face. He was an older man with gray hair, a clean face with green eyes that sparkled. He gave a sharp salute to the crew. He wore a four-pocket white shirt, surfer shorts, and bare feet. He came over to Lola. He patted several of his pockets to find something.

"They're on the top of your head," Lawanda said.

Rich ran a hand through his unruly gray hair and captured his wire-rimmed glasses. The crew all smiled at one another. Rich took Lola's hand and kissed it. He lifted it, so she stood.

"Welcome aboard, Lola," he said and looked her over. "Size two. Perfect."

Rich let go of her hand and took a seat where Arleen filled a plate. He thanked her. He took a bite, added syrup from a jar, and poured a glass of the protein drink. He chewed, drank, and swallowed before getting down to business.

"We designed the boat so that the keel swings up into a pocket in the middle of the hull. We put it down to prevent crabbing, going sideways." Rich paused in thought.

"With the swing keel up, this boat draws six feet at the waterline." Rich looked at the attentive faces one at a time. "We are currently sitting in four feet of water. There's a hole in the hull near the batteries and engines the size of Gus's *arse* with a coral head stuck up one foot inside the boat. We hit it pretty hard when we landed. There isn't enough room to patch it from inside. I have a patch that we can use to seal it from underneath once we are off the bottom. Someone will have to go underneath the hull and hold the patch in place while we use long screws to secure it from inside. Any questions?"

"What about the tides?" Mo asked.

"Low now but coming in," Rich answered. "According to the latest data, we'll have an increase of three and a half feet in four hours."

"Enough to float your boat," Arleen said, and they all laughed, but it was quick.

"We have a plan," Rich said. "Simone will fill you in individually."

No one at the table laughed. They could tell by how Rich cleaned his glasses with a napkin that it was not going to be easy. They took a deep breath collectively. Lola was drawn into the team. She had no idea of her part, but she knew she could do it. They all knew they could do it whatever it was.

They were all up from the table at once. Some grabbed a last bite and a swig of the shake. They were up the stairs and on deck, heading for the back of the boat. Simone was on the bridge flipping switches.

The transom at the back of the boat lowered to water level forming a platform large enough to hold the tender, an open boat large enough to hold the entire crew. It had been stored inside a utility room behind the transom and inside the hull that held dive gear and various pieces of equipment that Lola didn't recognize. There was also a silver bodysuit hanging with the other wet suits.

Lola guessed that it was a size two.

LOLA

Gus and Mo rolled the tender out onto the floating transom, careful to raise a large outboard engine on the back. They pushed the boat off the rollers into the water and tied it off next to Simone's dinghy. They lowered the motor but slightly brought it up when a swell bounced it off the shallow sand.

"Lola, come to the bridge," Simone called over a loudspeaker.

Franco and Lawanda were already in the water with dive masks on. Rich followed Lola as they climbed the stairs to meet with Simone. Arleen was still in the galley cleaning up after breakfast.

The bridge was a control room with large ports that looked out on the forward deck. There were also windows to the sides and back covering the aft deck. There were video screens across the control panel and instruments flickering to life.

"Simone and I designed this ship," Rich said. "It's part of an international fleet that documents sea life. My Foundation for Human Survival financed building it for shallow water reef exploration. *National Geographic* endorsed us in exchange for the first refusal of all of our work products. That gives us access to almost every country in the world."

"Only Cousteau had greater acceptance internationally," Simone said. "He was the father of environmentalism. He was a hero for the earth. We continue his work."

"Who's manning the bilge pumps?" Simone said, surveying all hands on deck and Arleen in the galley.

"I better get back down," Rich said. He looked at the instrument panel. "All systems go. We're able to pump it empty as long as that coral head is stuck in the hole. Ta ta for now."

He was gone.

LOLA

Simone motioned Lola to the screens. She pointed to one that was blank.

"Every mask has a camera and a light," Simone said. "There are cameras at vantage points on the boat. Rich also brought a drone with a camera. I can see all I need from here as well as control the engines and steering of the boat with that joystick or the 'old school' wheel."

She showed how the knob on a stick controlled direction and thrust. She pointed to a screen that showed Gus and Mo in the tender moving it out into deeper water behind the stern. Other screens showed the view from Franco and Lawanda's masks.

"When the tide rises above the coral head, Gus and Mo will swing us onto a smooth sand bottom where we can patch the hole from underneath. There should be about a foot and a half clearance from the bottom once we swing the keel up. The hull is covered with a Teflon-like paint that one of Rich's companies invented. No barnacles."

Lola was fascinated by the technology. Rich was in the bilge, stuffing rags in the space around the coral head. There was a blank screen.

"That's you," Simone said. "When you wear the silver bullet mask, I will be able to see everything you see. You'll have a bud in your ear so you can hear what's happening. We are all connected."

"What am I supposed to see?" Lola asked.

"The bottom of the boat," Simone said. "At high tide, we will have about a foot and a half clearance. Gus is too big. Lawanda is too pregnant. Rich is too old. Mo can free dive four hundred feet in the open sea, but he gets claustrophobic in tight spaces. "

"What about Arleen?" Lola asked.'"She won't fit into the suit. She's a size four." Simone laughed. "And we can't afford to lose her."

"So, I'm expendable," Lola said.

LOLA

"No, you're right for the part." Simone put her arm around her and kissed her on the head. "It's perfectly safe. We'll be watching you the whole time. You'll be using the hookah compressor with a long hose, so you won't have anything to get you stuck. No air tank."

"Stuck!" Lola said. "Stuck where?"

"Under the boat," Simone said. "Once we are above the coral, there will be too much water for the pumps to handle, so we have to put a patch on from the outside before the batteries and engines are flooded, and we'll be dead in the water. You'll swim under and put the patch in place and come right back out. Franco will be recording the entire thing for the movie."

"Dead in the water" was the phrase that echoed inside Lola's head.

"I know this is all new to you," Simone said. "I can do it if you don't want to. But we won't be able to use the recording. I could never get that silver suit on."

Lola looked at the white-haired angel in white. She was lean and strong, but the hand on her shoulder had arthritic nubs like she had seen on Popo's hands around his gun. Lola took a deep breath and exhaled anxiety.

"I can do it," Lola said.

Lola and Lawanda were in the utility hold where the tender had been stored. Franco was testing his camera and lights. He wore a full wet suit, and his mask covered his face. He pulled it up on top of his head after testing the light and camera on the mask. There was a larger camera in his hands with larger, brighter lights attached to both sides. As soon as the ship was afloat, he would view the bottom of the hull and the damage. He put down his equipment and stepped off the transom into the water that came up to his chest.

"It isn't very deep," Lawanda said. "Let's get you dressed and hooked to the hookah so you can get used to it. Have you ever used one before?"

"No," Lola said.

Lola took the silver bullet from its hanger and unzipped the front down to the crotch. She only wore a brief bikini that Lawanda had given her. Size two.

"Let me help you with that," Lawanda said. "Do the legs first and the feet. It's the best way I found to do it."

"I feel guilty that I'm taking your place," Lola said as she followed Lawanda's instructions.

"Not a problem," Lawanda said. "Getting pregnant was the best thing that ever happened to me. Or else I'd be doing what you're going to do. Then the arms and the hood."

"I saw a baby born in the middle of the hurricane," Lola said. "It was a miracle."

"Now the mask and regulator. We don't need your headset now," Lawanda said. "The switch for the lights and camera are on the left side of the mask. I'll switch on the compressor so you can breathe."

Lola had the regulator at the end of a long white hose in her mouth. She gave a thumbs up. The compressor was switched off, and she took out the mouthpiece to breathe. She watched Lawanda put on a tank and mask. Lawanda had a ripped body.

"I used to be a swimsuit model," Lawanda said. "It paid my way through college where ' got a Master's in Marine Biology. It's also how I met Franco. He was doing a photo shoot for *Sports Illustrated*. Our eyes met, and we connected. Love at first sight."

LOLA

She took Lola's hand and led her to the edge of the transom, where they sat down with their feet in the water before they put on their fins. Lola's were silver.

They could see the seagrass and sand below. Lola could hear the compressor running. She bit on the mouthpiece as they both slid over the edge.

The water only came up to Lola's chin. Four feet and rising. Lawanda bent over and ducked below to lead the way. Lola followed. She noticed Lawanda had a knife strapped to her lower leg. Lola dropped down to her knees, and Lawanda turned to check on her.

Thumbs up.

Kicking the fins stirred the sand, so they pulled themselves along the bottom with their hands as they looked at the blue hull on the sand.

Lawanda took the knife from her leg and used it as a pointer. There was life on the bottom in the grass. Small silverfish. She picked up a large conch shell to show Lola the creature inside. They heard the sound of a motor behind them. They could see the bottom of the tender as it tied up to the transom. There was Franco when the lights came on with his camera recording them. He was lying flat on the sand. His lips were moving behind the mask that fully covered his face. They couldn't hear him. Lola had not put in her earbuds, and Lawanda was ignoring him.

They all stood up when he turned off the lights. All heads were above the water. Lola had to stand on the tips of her fins to keep her chin above the water. Lawanda floated on her back. Franco had no problem. He was taller.

"How was the hookah," he asked Lola.

"Fantastic," Lola said. "No tank. No weights. I felt like a silver eel."

108

LOLA

"You are right for the part," Franco said. "I got some good movies with Lawanda. I think you're ready for the big scene in about an hour when the tide comes in. You know you will have to go under the ship."

"I'm preparing mentally," Lola said. "I explored a cavern once, and there were some tight spaces to get into the main chamber. I wasn't scared, but I had a guide with me."

"We'll all be with you the whole way," Franco said. "We can talk to each other, but you won't be able to talk because of the hookah. But you will be able to hear if you need to get out in a hurry."

"Don't worry," Lawanda said. "Nothing will go wrong."

They went back to the transom, and Gus was there to handle the equipment and help them out of the water. He was standing on the bottom, and the water was only up to his chest. Mo was in the tender with a thick braided rope that Arleen tied to a big cleat on the back of the ship.

"Keep the silver bullet on," Gus said. "If you get hot, jump in the water. Do you want to come up and rest before the big event? We've got about an hour until it's up to my chin."

"I think I'd rather just swim for a while to get loosened up," Lola said.

Lawanda handed her a mask with a snorkel. Lola floated on the surface to clear the mask and test the snorkel. With a kick of her silver fins, she was gone. She looked to the side at the blue hull about a foot below the waterline. She remembered what Simone had said about moving the ship. But the only phrase that echoed was "Dead in the Water."

Lola directed her attention to the feel of the sea against her silver suit. Slick as an eel. The fresh salt air came through the snorkel. The sound was from bubbles she expelled. She could stretch her arms and stroke, finish and glide. The grass below waved to her. Sunlight made changing patterns all around her. The sea was alive. She was alive. She remembered a line from a Hemingway book, not Ernest but one of his granddaughters, Lorian.

"Life, I love you so much."

That was just before the character died.

Lola swam back to the platform and held her breath the whole way. No problem. The water had risen far enough that even on her tiptoes with fins, it was up to her nose. She was a little over five feet tall. She wanted to get ready ahead of time to put her attention into the task at hand. Patch that hole.

Gus had brought a square sheet of plywood onto the platform. It was painted the blue of the hull. He was drying it with a blow dryer. He touched the board at various spots until his fingers came back clean. Satisfied, he turned it over and set an orange and red can with a stainless steel spatula from the galley on the clean side.

"Do you think you can lift this," Gus asked Lola after she had pulled herself onto the platform. "It's five by five by three-quarters thick. Rich took it from under his mattress. He said his doctor recommended it for his bad back."

Lola bent her knees and squatted down to grab it under one side. It was heavy. She dropped it and tried again. She could lift it to one side, but she knew she could never carry it. It was too big. She dropped it.

"Don't worry, *Langostina*." Gus laughed. "Big strong man will put it in the water, little sister. It will probably float. Lawanda has an extension boat hook to move it into place. You'll only have to lift it against the hull where the hole is until they screw it into place from inside. Do you think you're down for that?"

LOLA

"I'm down. I can do it," Lola said. "But I'm going to need a shovel."

"A shovel!" Gus said.

"I'm going to dig a hole under the hole in the hull, so I'll have room to work." Lola remembered Manuel, the long-haired motherfucker, and their talk as they walked the *Malecon*.

"Good idea," Gus said. He went into the utility room and returned with a dark green handle with a spade and a spike folded down onto it.

"My father has one of those from his time in the service," Lola said. "He called it an entrenching tool."

"You never know when you're going to need it until you need it," Gus said.

Lola took the tool and opened both spade and spike. There was a collar at the top of the handle that she turned to keep them in place. She put it down beside the plywood sheet.

"It works for me," Lola said.

"It better," Lawanda said. She had stayed in the background while Gus schooled Lola on the mission. "Don't forget these earbuds. You'll be able to hear us in case we see a problem. But since the Silver Bullet is on the hookah, you can't talk to us."

"But don't worry." Franco had come to the platform with his lights and camera. He raised his mask, and his face was above the water. "The Silver Bullet has superpowers according to the script."

"So I'm a stunt double," Lola said. "Whose going to play me in the movie?"

"Meryl Streep," Lawanda said. "Isn't she in every movie?"

"Coming down. I'm closing the panels," Simone's voice came over the loudspeaker.

They were quiet as the motors spun and the panels returned to complete the deck. Lola sensed apprehension in Simone's voice.

LOLA

Everyone put on their dive masks. Lola took the buds from Lawanda and put them in her ears. Franco and his camera disappeared along the starboard side to Lola's right. Lola put the mouthpiece from the hookah in her mouth after she wet her lips with her tongue. She pulled a deep inhale. It worked. She lowered herself into the water that was now over her head.

The water was clear. The ship still rested on the bottom. It seemed to move a little with a small swell. The lights from Franco's camera lit up the hull and the grass long enough for Lola to lay on her side and see the coral head before the boat settled back onto the sand. The blue plywood now floated above her.

Gus: "We need to get it under the hull. Not at the waterline."

Arleen: " I have some weights from my dive belt."

Simone: " First, take it around to Franco. It's a shorter distance to the keel."

Franco: " No good. The coral head is in the way."

The tide had lifted the ship high enough, so it did not settle back down on the sand. Lola could see it all. The hull, the grass, and the sand. She popped up next to Lawanda and the plywood patch. The red and orange can was gone, and a yellow slime had been spread along the edges. There was a bare spot in the middle where Arleen had put two lead weights.

Gus: " Don't get them next to the UPC."

Lawanda: " Underwater patching compound."

LOLA

Lola took the entrenching tool from the platform. "On the next big swell, I want to do a test run," she said.

Lawanda: "She wants to do a test run."

Simone: "Smart girl. I'm watching what's coming in. I'll let you know when one is big enough. It's ten meters to the hole. Thirty feet."

Half the length of my grandmother's lap pool, Lola thought. She couldn't count how many times they had swum the entire length and did a flip turn and swam back on one breath. She lowered herself until she was flat on the bottom between the two large ship's propellers.

Rich: " I drilled some long screws through the hull. You should be able to see them once we are off the coral. The higher we get, the more water is coming in. This will have to be quick once we are free."

Simone: "Here's a good one, Lola. Go. Lawanda put that patch on the bottom and push it along with her."

Lawanda: "Too much sand stirred up for the UPC."

Franco: "I see her. Recording. She looks great."

Lola knew that slower movement used less breath. A steady frog kick with the spade cutting a trench in front of her brought her to the coral head that had thrust up through the hull. There was no room to dig a hole.

Franco: "She's behind the coral next to the keel."

Simone: "Mo, are you ready on the port side?"

113

LOLA

Mo: "Tied up and ready to tug."

Simone: "It will have to be at least ten meters for the hull to clear the coral and give Lola a clear sand bottom."

Mo: "On your orders."

Simone: "Gus, go pull up the bow anchor. When we're clear, I'll pull up the swing keel and drop it back to stop us. Mo, go slowly."

Mo: "On your orders."

Rich: "I'm going to need something to fill this hole once the coral head is out."

Gus: "Bow anchor in the pocket."

Arleen "I have a purple yoga mat."

Simone: "Here comes the big one."

Lola had turned back and was waiting under the platform. She could feel the sea rise. She could see the hull lift.

Simone: "Mo, go!"

Mo: "Aye, aye, Captain."

Arleen: " Here's the mat. I can lay on it."

Rich: "It's not wide enough. Gus, come here. I need you."

LOLA

Gus: "On my way. I have to bend down. It's a lot easier for you little people."

Rich: "Put your arse in that hole."

Arleen: "All the way."

Rich: "Good job. As long as the bilge pumps keep up with the overflow."

Simone: "Lola, look at the hole. Lawanda, push that board in."

Lawanda: "Way ahead of you. It's between Lola and the coral."

Rich: "I can see her light. I've run out of towels."

Franco: "She's digging a hole under the purple mat."

Lola had begun to swim as soon as she saw Simone had dropped the swing keel to steady the boat. Franco's lights lit up the hull. When she reached the purple mat bulge above her, she stopped. She dug as deep as the spade would reach and as wide as her arms could reach. The plywood patch was there. There was enough room to turn and remove the weights from the middle of the board. It started to float. She lay on her back and pulled it over her. She had to stretch her arms up to place them against the purple bubble. She moved the board to cover the steel screws that she could see in the light from her face mask. She could hear the sound of power tools.

Franco: "I got it all."

Gus: "Let me out of here."

LOLA

Arleen: "Two more screws."

Mo: "Steady she goes."

Simone: " Rogue wave! "

Lola turned on her stomach and looked back at the way she had come in, half the length of her grandmother's lap pool. She would take a deep breath and swim out. She had her shovel beside her. The escape route got larger as the boat's back end was raised by the wave and lifted the hull until the swell passed her. Then the bottom dropped out as the wave continued toward the beach. The hull came down on top of her. She could feel her silver suit and the Teflon bottom slide against each other. She grabbed her shovel and went for that deep breath.

Lola pulled on the air hose. It slid easily beneath the hull and then stopped.

No air!

From her mask light, she could see it was under the keel. She knew how long she could hold her breath. She didn't know how long she could go without air.

Simone: "Did anybody get that? Lola, are you alright?"

Franco: "I got it all. Let me run it back slowly. Okay. She was in the hole. The hose floated under the keel."

Simone: "Mo, pull some more. We have to get off that hose."

LOLA

Mo: "I'm on my way. I was on my way to pull up the stern anchor. I'll get off to the side. It'll take a minute."

Simone: "We may not have a minute."

Lola had enough room in the hole to slide the shovel in front of her pointed to the escape route. Her light showed only a sand wall with ridges where she had cut out the hole. She tightened the collar on the spade and cut into the wall. Her heart was pounding so loud in her ears she couldn't hear the crew chatter. As the sand fell away, she saw something like a snake come toward her. She went to push it away. It was a braided rope. She grabbed it with her silver gloves. It was too slippery to hold. She wrapped the rope around the spade and the spike. The rope pulled the entrenching tool. She grabbed the handle and held on for dear life.

Never give up.

The Silver Bullet between the Teflon hull and the slick seagrass slithered toward the sliver of light half a pool length in front of her. Her chest burned. Her ears rang. A stingray swam next to her. She got a breath from the hookah as she popped up between the two propellers where Lawanda was waiting.

Lawanda: "She's out!"

Simone: " Clear the stern. I'm going to spin us around and get us out of here. We're crossing the bar!"

Rich: "It worked. We're high and dry."
Franco: "Which way are you spinning? I want to get this. Lola, can you go back under? Just swim across in front of the keel as it goes up."

117

LOLA

Lawanda: "She says she won't do it with the hookah."

Franco: "Continuity. Be sure she takes that shovel."

Lawanda: "Let me cut the end of that rope."

Gus: "You saved my arse, *Langostina*."

Gus had jumped in and put Lola on his hip. His face was still above the water while she and Lawanda were in over their heads. He walked around to where Franco was recording. Arleen, in all her glory, jumped in.
"That was close," Arleen said. "But I knew you would be alright."
"You sound just like my big brother," Lola said.
"Be sure to give us his cellphone number," Arleen said.
Lola laughed.

Simone: "All clear ."

Gus: "Fire it up, dude."

The engines came to life.

Rich: " All systems go."

Franco: "Hold it until the silver bullet passes the keel."

Simone: "I can see it on the feed from her mask camera. Go now while there is a calm."

Lola was free of the hookah. She had only her silver face mask and the shovel. The severed rope was still caught around the spade and spike. Lola took a deep breath, dipped beneath the waterline, and found a well-lit path to the swing keel in the center of the hull. She watched as it swung back up into the place it came from. She was out the other side, did a flip turn, and swam directly into the camera.

Simone: "Forward on the port. Back on the starboard."

Lola treaded water with her fins as they watched Simone back off enough, so the bow passed in front of them as the ship turned and faced out to sea. Lawanda was holding on to Franco, who had shut down recording. Gus stood above it all. Arleen floated on her back next to Lola.

"That was close," Arleen said. "I would have wet my pants."

"If you had any," Gus said.

As the *Bob Marley* crossed the bar, Mo came to them in the tender. First, he helped Franco put the camera onboard. Then Gus helped with the others.

"Weren't you scared?" Arleen asked Lola.

"I was too busy," Lola said. "I never thought about death until I popped up. I felt like I was born again."

"Well, here's part of your umbilical cord," Lawanda said. She handed Lola the end of the rope she had cut and unwrapped from the tool. "It's kind of slippery. It feels more like hair than hemp."

Lola looked at the rope end. It reminded her of Manuel walking away on the *Malecon*. There was a knot at the end.

"Great job," Simone said over the speaker. "Rest up."

Rich said, "Tomorrow is the big day."

"What was today?" Lola said.

"Rehearsal," Franco said.

LOLA

PART EIGHT

"Lola, please come to the bridge," Simone called over the loudspeaker.

Arleen helped Lola out of the Silver Bullet suit and gave her a sarong and a T-shirt with a picture of Wonder Woman on the front.

"I want to get one with your picture on it," Arleen said. "You're my hero."

"I wouldn't have done it," Lawanda said.

"Not with that belly," Gus said.

"Not with that belly," Lawanda said and poked Gus in the stomach.

"Careful," Gus said. "I'm having twins."

"Triplets," Mo said as he tied the tender to the stern.

"An Alien," Franco said. "Did anybody see that movie?"

"What is *Alien*, Alex?" Lola said.

"What is *Jeopardy*?" Gus said.

Lola gave him a high five.

"I'm sorry I couldn't move the boat before you came up," Mo said.

"Lola to the bridge," Simone called again.

The bridge was the control room for all activities. There were instruments for running the ship. There were also monitors for all the cameras that the crew wore. There was the old school wheel to steer and the joystick. Simone was at the wheel as they headed for deeper water.

"Gus, drop the bow anchor," Simone spoke into her handheld radio. "Now. Good boy. Well done. All engines stop."

Lola had climbed the steps and stood quietly behind Simone, watching her in command. She watched her check the instruments. Then she flipped a switch, and the monitors came to life. Each one showed a different view of the same scene.

"Look at what you did today." Simone brought Lola to the helm.

"That's me with the shovel!" Lola said as she watched Lawanda help her with the hookah. "I am the Silver Bullet. Down I go."

"That's what you saw." Simone pointed to another screen that showed the boat's underside with a stingray swimming toward a light where the coral head punctured the hull.

LOLA

"The space looked much bigger to me," Lola said.

"This next one is Franco's view," Simone said. "You swam just with your fins. Then it gets too blurred to see you."

"There's Rich stuffing towels around the coral head as water floods in. He's quite calm."

"Here, Mo pulls the boat away from the coral head."

"Rich calls for Gus. Gus squeezes into the bilge."

"That's Arleen's camera as Rich seats Gus in the hole to slow the flow. You can see how it worked."

"Franco's view is blocked by the coral and stirred up sand."

"That's me digging my escape hole," Lola said. "See the shovel?"

"There's Lawanda putting her head down to see you. As she pushes the board in with the weight to keep it down," Simone said.

"Now it clears up," Lola said. "I can see the board and the weights that I take off, and the board floats over me."

"Now Franco's view," Simone said. "As the wave lifts the hull, and you push the board up against the hull."

"I had to extend my arms all the way up to hold it while they screwed it in place," Lola said.

LOLA

"Those healing hands," Simone said. She then held her breath at the next scene from Franco as the boat came down on top of Lola.

"I learned about the escape hole from Manuel," Lola said. "Then my air was cut off, and you can see the shovel blade and the rope I wrapped around it."
"I don't see the rope," Simone said.
"Too much sand," Lola said.

"Franco's view is still blocked until the boat rises and you are gone." Simone continued.

"There I am on Lawanda's camera," Lola said. "I popped right up with a breath of air when the boat moved off my hose. You can see her cutting the rope that pulled me out."

"I don't see the rope," Simone said.

"I still have the piece of rope that was wrapped around my shovel," Lola lifted her T-shirt, and a length of rope was tucked into the waist of her sarong.
"It looks more like hair than any fiber rope I know," Simone said. "It's a miracle you made it out."

"I never gave up," Lola said. "I guess I'm just lucky."

"Not luck," Simone said. "The angels are watching over you."

"I didn't see any angels," Lola said. "Just a stingray and the rope."

"Angels sometimes have wings like a stingray," Simone said. "Or hair like Manuel."

LOLA

"Or Mo got a rope under the boat." Lola tried to understand. "And he pulled me out."

"Or Manuel, the long-haired motherfucker is an angel," Simone said.

"I don't know," Lola said.

Simone moved Lola into the chair beside the wheel, and she took the one next to her after turning off the screens. She set aside her radio. She had a small bottle in a holder of the command chair, and she took a quick swig and shuddered a bit before she talked to Lola.

"I know they all think I'm a crazy old lady," Simone said.

"They all praise you as a captain," Lola said.

"They think I'm crazy," Simone said, "because I'm always saying Philippe is coming tomorrow. They say he's dead. I say lost at sea in a plane crash. It doesn't matter. I say he's coming tomorrow because that was always the happiest day of my life. Knowing he would be back tomorrow. Not the day he got back. The day he got back was full of reports and communion with the crew and catching up and getting in the water where we would swim away from the longing and despair until he was too tired to do anything but lay down beside me and hold my hand until we slept."

"So he really doesn't come back?" Lola said.

"No," Simone said. "He really does come back. I can tell you because I see you believe in that realm beyond the sea with your hank of Manuel's hair."

124

LOLA

"I believe there is a lot I don't know," Lola said.

"You don't have to know to believe," Simone said. "It's called faith."

The deck panels had been raised to catch the last of the sun. In the galley, Arleen was preparing food. Gus was on the lowered transom in a speedo with a sling spear. Franco and Lawanda had gone to their cabin. Rich was nowhere in sight. Mo was on the bow with his prayer rug facing east bowed and reciting his evening worship.

Lola took her cellphone with her and found an isolated spot between the panels, and she called her mother on FaceTime.

"Your big brother keeps telling me you're alright," her mother said. "But I've been worried sick about you. Where are you, and what are you doing? When are you coming home?"

"I'm on an incredible boat with a great crew. I'm the Silver Bullet. I dress up in a silver suit, and they take videos of me underwater," Lola said.

"You're not doing drugs?" her mother said.

"No," Lola said. "The food is great. Arleen is a vegetarian cook. She is my boat sister. We do yoga together every morning."

"Arleen? Is that the girl your brother keeps talking about?"

"Yes," Lola said. "I'm in a movie for *National Geographic*. I'm the stunt double because I'm a size two. Lawanda was a size two, but she got pregnant, so they say I'm right for the part."

"You're not having sex, are you?"

"No," Lola said.

LOLA

"That Victor got my cell number and called. I told him you were at a swim meet," her mother said.

"I have his contact number and will call him back after I'm through here. Tomorrow is supposed to be the big day," Lola said.

"What does that mean?"

"I don't know yet," Lola said. "Everybody is excited about it."

"I had a strange feeling earlier today," her mother said. "I couldn't breathe. But it was just a bad dream. It is so good to hear from you. Can you send some pictures or a video?"

"I can show you the boat," Lola said, and she turned the phone to show the panels and the control tower where the bridge overlooked the deck.

"What are those?" her mother asked.

"Solar panels," Lola said. "The boat runs on electric."

"And who is that?" her mother asked as a tall, dark man in a speedo appeared coming forward.

"That's Mohammed," Lola said. "Mo, come to say hello to my mother."

"As-Salamu Alaykum," Mo said and bowed toward the phone.

"Inshallah," her mother said. "That's the only Arabic I know."

"That's all you need to know," Mo said. "It means 'God willing.'"

"He can free dive four hundred feet," Lola said.

"That's incredible!" Her mother was wide-eyed with admiration.

"It is nothing," Mo said. "What your daughter did is incredible. She saved the boat. Lola is our hero."

"It was nothing," Lola said.

"You can be very proud of this young woman," Mo said. "Wait till you see the video when we download it. "

"Later," Lola said, motioning Mo away. "Let me talk to my mother now."

"Asalamu Alaykum," Mo said as he backed away. "Remember Langostina. Tomorrow is the big day. The final day of shooting. Then you can go home."

"Inshallah," her mother said.

"Is everybody well at home?" Lola asked.

"Fine and dandy." Her father came into view. "We're all waiting for the return of our prodigal daughter."

There was a blast from the loudspeaker. "Clear the panels. Coming down. All hands on deck."

"I'll call you after we finish," Lola said. "Love you all. Over and out."

Lola could see Simone in the control room with a pair of binoculars, and she could hear the sound of an approaching motor. The panels had resumed their place in the deck. Off the port side, she saw a gray boat with a gun mounted above the steering station. Two armed men shouldered their rifles and prepared large blue fenders along the side as they came close and stopped.

Franco and Lawanda took lines from the gunboat and tied them to cleats on the port side. The gunboat turned off its engine. A man in a green uniform stood up.

LOLA

"Permission to come aboard," Diego said.

"Permission granted," Simone called down from the control room. "But no guns."

Diego said something to the two armed men on his boat, and they lowered their weapons and sat on the side of their boat. Mo was quick to greet them and gave them a pack of cigarettes, for which they were very grateful. He said something in Spanish that made them laugh. He then helped Diego up over the side and offered him a cold drink which he refused.

Lola had joined Simone on the bridge where Arleen was waiting with the silver suit. She helped Lola into it. Simone looked in a mirror in the bathroom and put on bright red lipstick. She opened the top two buttons on her white shirt. Arleen handed her a stack of papers as they climbed down to meet the policeman.

"These Latin men are all alike," Simone said and gave Lola a bright red smile. "Arleen, wait here until I need you."

Simone and the Silver Bullet came down to see Diego. He was all smiles when Simone flashed a red hello and wet her lips with her tongue. He removed his hand from the gun on his hip and reached out a hand for Simone.

"Diego," Simone said. "I am so glad to see you again. "What can we do to help?"

"I am here for Lola Lobo," he said.

"How are the people on the beach doing?" Simone said. "I'm sure you have more important things to do than take my leading lady away. We are on a very tight schedule. Tomorrow is our last day of shooting. Look here."

Simone got close enough to rub shoulders with Diego. She showed him the stack of papers. They all had official stamps on them.

"Ministry of Arts. Silver Bullet approved. Ministry of Defense. Approved. Ministry of Immigration. Approved. Ministry of Health. Approved. Prime Minister. Approved. And this one only has the signature of *El Presidente*. All approved for *National Geographic* and Silver Bullet. Lola Lobo is the Silver Bullet. Approved."

"But where are her papers?" Diego said.

"We all just went through a terrible hurricane," Simone said and put her arm around Diego's shoulder. "Things were lost and destroyed. I feel so sorry for the Cuban people. If there is anything we can do, I will personally be of service to you."
"Maybe someone at the Ministry could have made a mistake." Diego put his arm around Simone's waist. "They just have a few questions they want to ask her about the man she was photographed with on the *Malecon*."

"You mean Manuel the long-haired…" Lola started to say.
"He is just Manuel now," Diego said and returned to business. "Divers found him in a bubble in the ice hole of the overturned boat."
"Is he alive?" Lola asked.
"Alive and mad as hell," Diego said. "Someone cut off his hair, so now he is only Manuel."

Lola was speechless but felt the back of her silver suit where she had put the life-saving piece of rope that she kept with her since she came back aboard. She grabbed Simone's hand to steady herself. Diego put his hand back on his hip next to his gun to show who was in charge.

"Arleen," Simone spoke into her radio. "Please see if Rich is available."

Diego watched the naked girl come down from the bridge as she walked the length of the deck to the crew quarters. Arleen passed Lawanda and Franco, who were standing nearby. She smiled at Mo and the Cuban soldiers who shouted compliments as she passed. When she was gone below, Diego turned his attention to Simone, who wiped the lipstick from her mouth with a handkerchief and rebuttoned her blouse.

"I guess I've lost it," Simone said to Lola. "For love or money. We'll see what works best."

Rich came out right on cue. He was wearing a pair of cutoff shorts and a T-shirt with a picture of Mount Everest on the front. He showed a broad smile and extended his hand to Diego, who took it without hesitation.

"Mister Rich." Diego shook the hand vigorously.
"You know me?" Rich said.
"Everyone knows you," Diego said. "You are a great man."
"Thank you," Rich said.
"Are you here on business?" Diego asked.
"I'm on vacation," Rich said. "Away from the day-to-day pressures of how to spend my money."
"Or make more money," Diego said.
"As a matter of fact," Rich said, "I was thinking about setting up a Bitcoin mine in Santiago if I can find the right people who are honest and determined to complete the job."

LOLA

"I know many such people," Diego said.

"I'll be in touch with the Ministry of Finance when I get back to the office," Rich said. "In the meantime, here is what I have on me to help you and the people of this town who saved my leading lady. Lola Lobo."

Rich took a wad of paper money from his back pocket and handed it to Diego, who put it in his back pocket.

"I have to get back," Diego said. "I'll tell my boss that mistakes were made. Lola Lobo is a movie star. An actress. The Silver Bullet papers are all in order. Thank you for your cooperation. Good luck with your filming tomorrow."

Diego went back to his boat and crew, where Mo helped him down. He gave orders to his men. The boat started up. He turned back to the ship.

"You are a great actress," Diego said. "*Langostina!*"

When the Cuban boat had gone, Gus popped up out of the water.

"All clear?" Gus said.

"All clear," Simone said.

"We eat tonight," Gus said and raised his spear with a feast-sized grouper on the end.

Lola took a hot shower in Simone's room and found a sarong and T-shirt with a picture of Meryl Streep on the front. She laughed as she got dressed. Simone came in and started fussing about looking for this and that.

"You'll have to sleep somewhere else tonight," Simone said, looking in the mirror above her desk. She frowned. She smiled. She laughed out loud. "Tonight's the night."

LOLA

"I understand," Lola said and tucked the rope that saved her into the waist of the sarong. "Where should I sleep?"

"Just ask Arleen," Simone said. "She's slept with all of them. Now let me have some time alone. Enjoy that dinner that Gus caught."

"I don't know how I feel about eating fish. It upsets me," Lola said. "I've been with them so much they seem like family."

"There are things in life that you should be upset about," Simone said. "This is not one of them."

Arleen had found a large white table cloth that Lola helped her spread on the wide deck. There were utensils in a pile in the middle with six plates and linen napkins. Five plastic champagne flutes came next

"Only five?" Lola said.

"Mo doesn't drink alcohol," Arleen said. "And Simone said she won't be joining us."

"I don't drink," Lola said. "Maybe on special occasions."

"This is a special occasion," Arleen said. "And you are the guest of honor."

"Me!" Lola said.

"Rich said so," Arleen said. "You saved the ship. Just take a sip. I don't eat anything that had a mother, but I'll take a bite since Gus went to all this trouble. He's down below cleaning and grilling it. "She sniffed the air. "Maybe two bites. It smells so good. I made rice and quinoa with something green as a side. And I smell french fries."

"Where should I sit?" Lola said.

LOLA

"I'll get some cushions," Arleen said. "We're very informal and only eat at the table for breakfast and the day's briefing. I usually just prepare some dishes, and people passing through the galley take what they like and go where they want. When I make bacon, Mo sits upwind until it's gone. That's the only pork. Gus will eat anything and what is left over. Franco and Lawanda feed each other. So cute! Simone gets her own, and Rich lives on inspiration and peanut butter."

"How long have you been doing this?" Lola asked.

"All my life," Arleen said and gave a namaste to Lola, who returned it with a bow.

The grilled fish was on a platter in the middle of the table cloth. Rice and quinoa colored with broccoli spears were in bowls at both ends, as were the french fries. A bottle of catsup was available.

"Fish and chips, my favorite," Rich said as he came up and rested on a cushion.

Franco and Lawanda wore matching kaftans. Mo wore a long white robe. Gus wore his black and white kaftan that was much too short but respectable. Arleen wore Arleen.

"Who's the master of the sea?" Gus said, pointing to his feast.

"Goose, goose, goose," the crew responded, imitating how Simone pronounced Gus's name.

"Goostave, the provider," Gus said. "Brain food."

Mo said a prayer in Arabic.

"Amen," the crew responded and began to fill their plates. No one reached for the utensils. They ate with their right hand in the Arab fashion to please Mo.

Rich opened the bottle of champagne and filled the flutes. There was a pitcher of water that he poured for Mo. Rich raised his glass.

LOLA

"To my family at sea," Rich said. "And a special toast to Lola Lobo for saving the boat and this production. And a toast to tomorrow when we wrap this film."

"Inshallah," Mo said.

The rest said, "Amen."

There wasn't much talk but a lot of delightful sighs. The fish had been grilled, so the skin was crunchy and the meat tender. The fries were crisp and disappeared first. Mo had seconds on the fish and scooped the rice dish with two fingers. Arleen begged forgiveness from the vegan spirits and took another helping of fish until only the spine remained. Lola gave thanks and ate.

"Not too much," Lawanda said. "You still have to be a size two tomorrow."

"What a marvelous vacation," Rich said when the laughter stopped. "I am the luckiest man in the world."

"Second luckiest," Franco said and kissed Lawanda. "We are going to be married."

"When?" Arleen said.

"Tomorrow, after the shoot," Lawanda said. "If Captain Simone will perform the honors. Is that right, Rich?"

"Right as rain," Rich said. "Bite my tongue! No rain. Please, no rain."

Lola had taken a sip of champagne when the toast was made and now another sip thinking about tomorrow. She was ready. She could do whatever was needed. She secretly felt the hair rope tucked into her sarong.

LOLA

"Simone and I built this boat big enough so that the crew could have the same luxury as the captain," Rich said.

"Kingsize bunk," Gus said. "And seven-foot headroom. Sign me up forever, boss."

"That crazy old lady is going to marry us," Lawanda said. "I'd follow her anywhere. I love her."
"You would love her even more," Gus said, "if you had been on the bridge during the storm. I was there while you were all peacefully in your beds."

"It wasn't so peaceful," Mo said. "I prayed a lot."

"There was a storm?" Franco said. "Did you notice a storm, Lawanda?"
"Only you," Lawanda said.

"I was completely at ease with Simone at the helm," Rich said. "Even though I tightened down my escape hatch when I saw the white water coming over the top."

"We were in the curl," Gus said. "The tsunami was pushing us from behind, and the hurricane was on our nose. Head for the center and turn left is the normal tactic. But not Simone. She headed straight for the center eye where it was calmer, and we rode the eye until the surge caught up with us. It was a wall of water higher than the control room. When it started to break, she made a hard starboard turn, dropped the keel, and surfed the wave down the face, then into the curl through the tube and out the end as it closed out. She cut the engines as the wave passed us and stuck the landing on the sandbank before we were carried to the beach. I gave her a ten, but the Russian judges gave her a five because we landed on that coral head."

LOLA

"I had tied myself to the bow winch," Arleen said. "I saw the whole thing. It was magnificent."

"You're as crazy as she is," Lawanda said.

"You only get a chance like that once in a lifetime," Arleen said. "What's next?"

"Getting ready for tomorrow," Rich said. "Come on, boys, let's give Arleen a break and do the galley tonight. Gus, you wash, Mo, you dry. We'll take care of the leftovers. Franco, you clean up here and then prepare the shooting schedule for tomorrow."

Darkness preceded the moonless night. It would be up later. At the moment, the three girls lay on their backs, watching the stars pop up until the sky was full.

"Do you believe in life after life?" Lola asked. She took out her hair rope and waved it to the stars.

"There is only one life, and it is eternal," Arleen said. "There is no now. Only the past and the future flowing together to become a life that is."

"In Haiti," Lawanda said. "Where I was born, we have Voodoo. It is beyond comprehension. Sometimes the magic works."

"And sometimes the magic works," Lola said. She spoke to the hair rope. "Do you believe that a man could have traveled through the sea to save me?"

"What do we know?" Lawanda said as she looked at the starry night. "We are just a thought in infinity. Do you think there is more than our thoughts in the vast universe? One hundred years ago, if you told someone you could talk to and see your mother thousands of miles away, they would think it impossible. We know so little. As many times as I have studied the sea, I still don't know its secrets. Every time I learn something new. And that's only what I can see and hear."

"I can see and hear the boys down below," Arleen said.

"I guess they're through with the dishes," Lawanda said. "I had better go help Franco with tomorrow's shooting schedule."

"And tap Tommy on the head," Arleen said.

Lawanda got up and walked toward the front of the boat, where she found the open hatch to their room, swung her legs into the opening, and lowered herself down.

"Simone wants to be alone tonight," Lola said. "She said to ask you where I should sleep."

"I've slept with all of them," Arleen said. "Not sex, just sleep. I haven't had sex in three years. At least not with another person."

"Is that how long you've been on this boat?" Lola asked.

"Simone met me on an island where my last lover left me. He said I was too obsessed with cleaning. I lived in a cave on a beach and did housework for people during the day when I felt like it. Simone was looking for a stewardess for her boat when she saw me with a mop and bucket. It was love at first sight."

"She's very intuitive," Lola said. "It was the same with me."

"I tried to sleep with Mo one night," Arleen said. "He put a pillow between us and recited verses from the Quran. He said if we made love, he would have to marry me, and I was too old and not a virgin. You'd be perfect."

"What about Gus?" Lola wasn't ready to wed.

"He's a honey bear and a gentleman," Arleen said. "You can curl up safe and warm. Until he rolls over, and you're left hanging onto the edge of the bed."

137

LOLA

"So you usually sleep with Simone," Lola said.

"Until she falls asleep," Arleen said. "Then I get up, and I have the boat to myself."

"What do you do?" Lola asked.

"I dance in the moonlight," Arleen said. "Come on, dance with me."

"Do we need music?" Lola said as she stood up.

"Just listen," Arleen said.

They could hear the water moving past the hull. The wind sang with the air. There were the calls of distant birds and fish splashing in the water.

The moon began to rise.

Arleen took Lola's hand and led her through swirls, leaps, and bows. Together they danced the length of the boat from stern to bow. They looked at each other and laughed as they came to the four hatches open to the crew quarters. Arleen put a finger to her lips for silence as they spied upon them.

Mo's room was dark but for the light from his cellphone. He was talking in Arabic and laughing. They could hear the voice of a woman on the other end. Then a man and some interrupting children. Mo was happy with his life and at peace with his God.

Gus's hatch was open. A tablet with a movie playing lay on his chest. An empty champagne bottle lay at his side. His mouth was open, and his eyes were closed. His arms and legs were stretched out, and his feet hung over the bottom. No room at the inn.

LOLA

They could hear Lawanda's sounds and Franco's sighs. They didn't bother to look inside. They moved to where Rich's lights were on with a clickety-clack of computer keys.

"Ahoy mates," Rich said, looking up at them as they looked down at him and his laptop.

"Rich is the best," Arleen whispered. "He'll put you to sleep."

"What about you?" Lola asked Arleen.

"I'll get a mat and a sheet and sleep on deck," Arleen said. "I sleep in the air."

Rich was on his back, covered with a sheet. When he sat up, he reached the hatch and pushed it wide open. He moved to one side of the bed and put his computer on a night table. The room was big enough to have a couch, desk, and bathroom.

"Incoming," Arleen said and helped Lola through the hatch down onto the bed next to Rich. She blew Lola a kiss. She was gone.

"Excuse me," Lola said as she sat down. "I just need a place to get some sleep. It's been quite a day. I'm exhausted. Thank you, Rich."

"You can use the couch if sleeping next to me makes you uncomfortable," Rich said.

Lola looked over at the couch, and it seemed so far away. She felt quite comfortable where she was. After all, he was a billionaire. Something to write home about.

"You know who I am," Rich said, looking around for something he had misplaced.

"They're on your head," Lola said and held back a laugh.

"I have so much on my mind that I sometimes forget the little things." Rich put on his glasses and looked into the eyes of his new roommate. "You know who I am. Who are you?"

139

LOLA

"I am the Silver Bullet," Lola said. "I am Lola Lobo. I am *Langostina*."

"And what do you want?" Rich asked a question that seemed to be the story of his life since he became wealthy."

"I just want to get home to my family," Lola said.

"That's not a problem," Rich said. "After we finish tomorrow, I'm leaving. I'll take you with me to wherever you want to go."

"That would be wonderful." Lola relaxed and lay back on the bed.

Rich twisted and turned and let out an audible yet unintentional groan.

"Are you okay?" Lola asked.

"Just one of the benefits of age," Rich said. "Pain lets me know I'm still alive."

The sheet had slipped down to his waist. He was tan and muscular with white hair wherever he had hair on his head, chest, and arms. He always wore a smile.

"What do you want to do with your life?" he asked.

It was not the first time Lola was asked. She had thought about it but never found an answer. Life seemed to find something more immediate to do.

"There are so many choices," Lola said. "I find it best to just let my spirit guide me."

"You're a lot like me," Rich said. "Whatever I needed always came to me. I didn't need to search. I needed a Silver Bullet, and you showed up. My businesses have all come to me, and I took advantage and made money. Lots of money. That brought more businesses and more money. I spend more time spending money than making money."

"Not everybody has that problem," Lola said. "There are more poor people than wealthy people."

"And that takes up most of my time," Rich said. "To whom do I give?"

"Is that a problem?" Lola asked.

"Bigger than you think," Rich said. "Everybody wants something. But who are they, and what will they do? Do you know how many people I have employed to find the frauds and government grafters? It's not simply supply-and-demand like in business. It's surplus and need. Like the factory, Lawanda's father and I are trying to start in Haiti. Where governments are involved, money is an ice cube. After it goes through so many hands, by the time it gets to the need, all that's left are a few drops of water. So I finance projects like this boat to show the world that the sea is our neighbor, not a slave or a garbage dump. And now we're making money by doing a movie with *National Geographic*."

Lola was listening through the fatigue that soon overwhelmed her. She was fading fast. She heard him say something that brought her back.

"You better rest up for tomorrow ," Rich said.

There was a spattering of rain on the open hatch. It was opened wide, and a sheet and yoga mat came down, followed by Arleen. She stood between them and closed the hatch before she lay down.

"Hope you don't mind my dropping in," Arleen said.

"It's our pleasure," Rich said.

LOLA

"I'll tell you about what I saw in the morning Lola." Arleen was excited but tired.

"We all need our rest now," Rich said. "Tomorrow, Lola Lobo swims with the whale sharks."

LOLA

PART NINE

The sun hadn't yet risen. The deck was wet with early morning dew. There was no breeze, and the sea was flat. The boat was quiet.

Lola and Arleen took their yoga mats to the aft deck while Rich still curled up in his bunk. The rest of the crew was nowhere in sight. Simone's hatch was closed and showed no sign of movement.

"It's real," Arleen told Lola before they began. "I saw him. I heard him. He kissed me and pinched me on the butt. Definitely French."

"Are you sure it was Philippe?" Lola asked.

"Who else?" Arleen said. "I decided to sleep below Simone's hatch. It was open. I lay there a long time waiting and started to fall asleep. I heard a man say, '*J'e t'aime.*' I love you. I tried to look inside, but it was too dark. Then someone came up behind me and pinched me. I turned, and the instant I saw him, he kissed me on both cheeks. He said, 'We are all the sea. Liquid, vapor, and land.' And then he disappeared into the mist."

"Are you sure it wasn't all a dream?" Lola said.

143

LOLA

"Look at my butt," Arleen said. She turned to show a red mark, but the light was too dim. "Feel it."

Lola touched where Arleen pointed. There was a hot spot. She pulled back and began her salutation to the sun. There were some things beyond her understanding. She would clear her mind of the morning brain fog and settle into herself. The sun showed an arc of yellow light in the east above the sea, unblemished by clouds. The day had begun.

Arleen moved below to prepare the morning meal when Lola saw Simone come out of her cabin and dive over the side. She had not seen Lola. Simone swam away without much sound. Then Lola heard sobbing. She quickly dove in after her.

Lola swam to the shadow that betrayed Simone. They were two women alone in the sunrise. Simone was still sobbing but softer now. Lola touched her hand as they floated together.

"Sometimes a woman needs a good cry," Simone said. "Even if it's tears of joy."

"So you're alright?" Lola said.

"Right as rain," Simone said, bit her tongue, and they both laughed.

They swam back to the boat, where a ladder hung over the side. Lola climbed up first. Simone followed.

"Never leave the boat unless you have a way to get back on," Simone instructed.

"He was here last night?" Lola said.

"Without a doubt," Simone, who was naked, said. "Get into some dry things. Take one of my kaftans. It'll be a little big, but you won't need it for long. The Silver Bullet rides again today. Arleen will have the right meal for you. You'll be in the water most of the day. Franco will fill you in on what he wants before we find the whale sharks."

When Lola got to the galley, the deck panels and solar collectors were in place. Everyone was there but for Simone, who was on the bridge, moving out. Gus had already lifted the anchor and secured the tender to be towed. Rich was at the sink washing his hands,

"The drone is ready to launch," Rich told them as they selected food from the fruit and carbs Arleen had set out for them, along with the coffee that had been brewed by a timer that was set the night before.

Lola sat down at the table and took a sip of the green smoothie Arleen had made special for her. It tasted of banana oat milk and something green. It was refreshing and stimulating.

"Spirulina," Arleen said. "You're going to need some superpowers today."

"According to the satellite," Rich said. "There's a large spawning the size of an island about two hours from here. The whale sharks will feed on the released eggs and sperm. We will meet them. Franco will tell you what he wants between now and then. Good hunting!"

"Gus," Franco said. "I want you to ride shotgun on all of this in case anything unexpected happens. Mo, you'll scout the reef for what we shoot before getting to the whales. Lawanda will watch from above and communicate with the Silver Bullet if she spots something interesting for Lola. Lola, we're going to record you as you explore the reef."

"Do I have to wear the hookah?" Lola asked.

145

LOLA

"How long can you hold your breath?" Franco asked.

"How long would you like?" Lola was already feeling her superpowers.

The drone was about the size of a boogie board with a propeller mounted above each end. Underneath was a camera that was directed by controls on the bridge. It rested on wheels but had an automatically inflated life ring if it should land in the water. The transom had been lowered to sea level and cleared of anything that would get in the way once the props started to rotate. The electric engine whined, the props spun, and the drone called "Little Rich" rose into the air.

"The GPS is programmed and connected to the satellite," Franco said. "It will take some time for Simone to reach the spawning ground, so we have time to shoot along the reef until the drone picks up the whales. That will leave Simone, Rich, and Arleen on the *Bob Marley* while we take the tender. We will all be in communication through our cameras and headsets. Get into your gear, and let's become explorers."

Lola put on her Silver Bullet costume. Gus wore a tank with two regulators and carried his spear. Lawanda also wore scuba gear. Mo wore a speedo and a dive mask. Franco wore his tank and mask along with his camera and lights that he placed on the floor of the tender as Gus started the engine and released the bowline. Simone had slowed to a stop while the tender party boarded and drifted away from the big boat.

"Let the games begin," Simone said as she lowered the solar panels and increased speed.

LOLA

The tender followed the big boat until they could see a large reef that ran along the coast in shallow water with unlimited visibility. They could see the reef drop off a short distance toward the sea, where it became a wall that fell away into the big blue.

Franco was in the water with his camera first. Next came Lawanda beside him and then Gus with his spear. Lola waited on the side while Mo steered.

Franco: "Lola, I want you to fall back into the water and dive down as close to the reef without touching the white tip fire coral. Then swim along as far as you can on one breath. Lawanda will tell you if she sees anything for you to investigate."

"Ready when you are," Lola said and sat with her back to Franco, who had the camera above the surface to record her entrance. She saw Mo continually looking over the side and monitoring the depth gauge. She took a few small breaths and then a deep breath.

"Action," Franco said.

Lola flipped backward into the water and turned to face the camera before kicking her way down and swimming along not far from the surface where the colors of life burst out of the different shaped corals and radiant fish of all sizes and shapes.
She swam over tall orange Elkhorn corals and green Brain coral and yellow Staghorn corals and sea fans of red, purple, blue, yellow, green. Silverfish with blue stripes, white and blackfish with yellow stripes, a school of bluefish, Parrotfish in red, green, blue…
She needed to take a breath.

Lawanda: "Shark, below you on the sand. "

147

LOLA

Lola snorkeled on top until she saw the large gray shark. It had a tall, erect tail fin. Its dorsal fin moved only slightly, and its pectoral fins were motionless at its sides as it rested.

Lawanda: "Nurse shark. They don't bite. See how close you can get."

After a deep breath, Lola bent at the waist and put her head down and her feet up out of the water as she dove down to the shark. It sensed her approach and slowly moved away, with Lola following close behind until they were to the edge where the coral reef fell off into the sea. Time to come back up.

Franco : "Incredible! You're like a fish."

Lawanda: "A turtle. To your right."

Lola turned to her right, and a huge turtle came so close to her mask that she had to back off. It was brown, yellow, and green with a remora fish suckered to its shell. She tried to follow it but was distracted by a stingray crossing her path. Its wings waved as it ran along a white sand bottom between the larger corals. Swaying soft corals and tall white pillar corals were on both sides of her. She had taken dive lessons and even qualified for open water. This was different. It was a world of more life than a crowded city. Constantly revealing new shapes and colors.

Franco: "Keep going. I'm getting it all. Such natural clarity I don't need my lights."

Lawanda: "Moray eel in a cave to the left. Don't put your fingers in there."

LOLA

Lola dove to the cave where she saw the green head, menacing teeth, and eyes that watched her every move. A silverfish being chased by a bigger fish swam by the cave. Faster than a flash, the green head sprung out and caught the silverfish and withdrew to the cave.

Franco: "Got it. Fantastic."

Lawanda: "Octopus. Ahead of you. Same color as the coral."

Up again. Down again. Lola looked closely at the coral and couldn't see the octopus until it waved an arm at her. She went to touch it, but it shot away in a cloud of black ink.

Mo: "There is a canyon between two shelves about thirty feet down. Sandy bottom."

Franco: "Go for it, Lola. I'll get you from above."

Lola swam down between two coral walls. There was white sand on the bottom. She knew that she could fit through the narrow canyon. Driven mainly by her fins, she swam slowly along the path. It was breathtaking, and she had to twist and kick back up, avoiding the white tips and spiny black sea urchins.

Mo: "There's an arch in front of you. Franco, she can swim through it and out the other side."

Franco: "Wait for me to get down first to set up."

Lola floated while she watched Franco take the camera down to the bottom.

LOLA

Franco: "Action."

Lola swam down.

Down past Franco to the far side of a coral arch. She could see him on the other side. She waved and entered the space beneath the coral crescent. A barracuda was waiting at the top of the arch. She held her breath and slowly swam by, trying not to look at the sharp teeth sticking out of his jaws. She made it through.

Franco: "That was perfect."

Mo: "There's a school of fish just over the edge."

Franco: "On our way."

The edge of the wall dropped down so far that light filtered in, narrowing rays to what seemed infinity.

Franco led the way over the wall, and Lola followed him. When she saw that he was set up, she took another breath. It would be a long deep dive, but she could do it.

Once over the edge, she saw that the wall was alive with coral and fans. Fish of all kinds swam in out and around. The lights from Franco's camera brought out the vibrant colors that faded in the depths. Ahead of her was a large school of silverfish in the thousands, so thick that she could not see through to the other side or the end. Lola swam straight ahead into the school that flashed and reflected on her silver suit.

Lawanda: "Be careful. You can't see what might be coming on the other side."

150

LOLA

Lola swam ahead, brushing aside the silver croud as it fled past her away from ...

A shark coming face to face with her. They saw each other at the same time. Both were startled. Lola stopped. The shark turned and left a trail of poop as it was frightened away.

Gus: "You really scared the shit out of him."

Lola turned and raised her hand above her head so she wouldn't bump into the bottom of the boat. She looked up. It was a long way to the surface.

Lawanda: "You're at twenty meters, sixty feet. Can you make it?"

Gus: "I've got her covered."

Lola swam past Gus as he came to her aid. A simple thumbs-up. She continued her climb to the light at the surface, where she could see Lawanda waiting. It was a hard swim. Her breath was gone, but she knew to continue to blow out as her lungs expanded from the change in pressure. It was so far. Maybe too far. The length of her grandmother's lap pool. Keep kicking. Never give up. She had tears in her eyes when she reached a breath.

Air!

Mo: "Franco, you've been down long enough."

Lawanda: "Too long!"

Gus: "I'm on my way. I have enough air to get there. Half enough to bring both of us back up."

LOLA

Lola watched Mo drop a weighted line over the side, cut the engines, and dove down with only a mask. She watched as he swam past Gus and reached Franco, who was still recording on the descending wall. They both reached him. Gus after Mo.

Mo: "Franco, give me the camera."

Franco: "No! I have to get this. Leave me alone."

Lawanda: "He's got the rapture."

Lola could see Mo and Gus struggling with Franco. Mo took the camera. Gus grabbed Franco and pressed the button to inflate Franco's vest to lift him off the bottom. No good. No air. Gus took the regulator from his mouth and put it in Franco's mouth. Buddy breathing. Franco still resisting.

Gus: "Come on. We only have enough air to get up to fifty feet. He's going to need to decompress."

Lola saw them leave the bottom and begin a slow ascent. She saw Lawanda next to her, getting ready to go after them. Lola grabbed her arm.
"Give me your tank," Lola said. "You can't do this with the baby. Too deep. I can do it."

Lawanda resisted at first, but Lola already had unstrapped the tank from Lawanda's back and pulled the regulator from her mouth. Lola put the tank under her arm and bit down on the regulator. Air! She climbed down the rope that Mo had deployed. He showed an okay sign as he passed her with the camera going up. No bubbles were coming up from Gus and Franco. They met halfway. Gus passed Franco to Lola after taking a breath from her tank and headed up.

Lawanda: "I'll tell you when to stop and decompress. Franco, stay with us."

Gus: "He didn't want to leave. He wanted to stay there forever until Mo showed him his air gauge. Empty."

Lawanda: "Lola, stop. Hold onto the rope there for three minutes."

Lola looked at her gauges. Fifty feet. Air at the red line. Three minutes.

Lawanda: "Stop again at fifteen feet."

Franco: "I have to get it all. So beautiful. Why are you taking me away?"

Lola: "Let's not waste our breath."

They hung together in silence. Lola faced Franco, who held her by the hips as she moved the regulator from one mouth to the other. There was also silence from above. They all waited for five minutes just to be sure the nitrogen and helium had dispersed from his blood.

Mo pulled Franco in and laid him on the floor of the tender. Lawanda was quick to his side. She removed his mask and dive gear. She ran her hands through his hair and kissed him on his face and hands.

Lola grabbed Mo and Gus by the hands, and they lifted her into the tender. She pulled the silver hood off her head and shook out her hair. She felt the back of her suit where she carried the hair rope. It wasn't there. She had forgotten it.

"We've spotted the whale sharks," Simone's voice came over the radio.

Catching up to the *Bob Marley* was against a strong current that Gus navigated by quartering the incoming swells and racing down the back. Lola sat on a life jacket to cushion the bumps. Mo lay flat on a cushioned seat by the transom with his eyes closed and his hands holding prayer beads. Lawanda was at Franco's side on the floor, rubbing his hands. His eyes were open, but there was no telling what he saw.

"I got the most incredible pictures on the wall," Franco said. His mind was still one hundred feet below the surface. Lawanda brought him up.

"Hold on!" Gus yelled. "Sorry!"

The tender slammed down after plowing through a white cap. It jolted everyone. Franco sat up. His eyes focused on Lawanda. He spoke to her in French. She translated for Lola.

"I love you, Lawanda," Franco's first words. His memory crept back. "I love Mo. I love Gus. I love the Silver Bullet. I love life!"

"It's a team sport," Gus said. "One for all. All for one."

"What is the *Three Musketeers*, Alex," Lola said and felt the empty space where her hair rope should have been.

"What is *Jeopardy*?" Gus said. "I spent a month in the hospital watching television after I got bent."

"Bent," Lawanda said. "The bends. It's what happens when you dive at depth. Decompression sickness. Nitrogen bubbles form in the

154

joints. It is very painful, and sometimes the side effects last a long time. Confusion. Loss of coordination. Memory loss."

"I had it all," Gus said. "I was in the decompression chamber five times because of my size. Also, the nurses were pretty, and the food was good, and I needed a vacation after working off an oil rig in the Gulf for two years."

"You're alright now?" Lola asked.

Gus didn't answer at first, needing to clear a wave. He looked around at Franco and Lola. He gave a big smile.

"So far, so good," Gus said. "I haven't lost anybody yet."

"Inshallah," Mo said.

"Thar she blows," Gus said when the Marley came into sight.

The big boat had stopped with the transom down, and the drone returned. Rich and Arleen were folding back the propellers and storing it back inside.

Simone oversaw everything from the bridge. The tender pulled alongside the floating transom and put out fenders while everyone disembarked. Franco came last with Lawanda holding his arm for support.

"All went well?" Rich asked.

"Like clockwork," Gus said.

"I was with Simone while we got the pictures from your cameras," Rich said. "That was quite some free dive, Mo."

"One hundred feet." Mo laughed. "I do that before breakfast."

"And Lola, you were quite calm considering," Arleen said and helped Lola take down the top part of the silver suit. "Don't take it all off. In half an hour, the whale sharks will be alongside."

LOLA

"That current is pushing the spawn right into their mouths," Rich said. "We should get some really exciting footage before I leave today."

"You are leaving," Lola said.

"Right after the wedding," Rich said.
"I'm going with you?" Lola asked.
"I don't see why not," Rich said. "This is the last day of shooting. We won't need you after that."

Lola caught her breath. She would leave. In a way, she didn't want to go. Like her *Familia Cubana*, the crew had become very close to her. There was a feeling that they depended on each other. She belonged. They had needed her in more ways than one. She was the Silver Bullet.

Arleen had prepared nutritional drinks for all of them. Franco was hesitant at first, but Lawanda convinced him he needed it if he was going to shoot the whale shark. He drank slowly and found his camera gear, and checked the battery. He was returning to his life before the rapture.

"Should you go down again so soon?" Lola looked him over, especially his eyes. They were clear. He moved slow but sure.
"He'll only shoot from the surface," Lawanda said. "The whale sharks will be right up top with those large mouths open sucking up all that food from the spawn pushed in by the current. Lola, it will be a pleasant swim. They are not dangerous. They have hundreds of small teeth, but they don't bite."

"I've always wanted to swim with them," Lola said.

"Me too," Lawanda said. "I don't want to miss this chance. You never know when you'll get this chance again. It is a dream of every marine biologist. "

"I don't want you to go," Franco said. "In your condition."

"My egg and sperm will be right at home in this spawn," Lawanda said.

"Just don't get too close to the mouth," Franco said.

"Yes, Uncle Frank," Lawanda said and kissed him on the nose. "I'm my own boss. We're not married yet. "

"Look off the starboard," Simone said. "I can see at least three of them. Two big females. One smaller male followed them. One female has a calf. Get ready. I'm heading for the pod!"

The largest of the whale sharks and the *Bob Marley* moved closer together. Simone maneuvered alongside the animal nearly as long as the big boat. It was dark gray covered with white spots and horizontal lines across its back. The head was blunt, and three ridges ran parallel to a large dorsal fin, a small dorsal, and a tall tail that stuck high out of the water.

Looking down from the ship, Lola thought it looked just like the nurse shark she had seen earlier, only a thousand times larger. Lola moved down to the transom and zipped up her silver suit. Lawanda was already in scuba gear. Franco had his camera and swim gear ready to go. Gus stood by with his spear and gear. Mo was in the tender that was being towed. He untied and drifted back to start the motor and drive to the other side of the whale shark far enough away not to scare her but close enough to respond if called.

Arleen had her mask on. Rich was in the control room with Simone monitoring the pictures coming in from all the crew's cameras. Lola waited for instructions from Franco.

LOLA

Franco: "Lola, I want you to use the hookah. I want to get a shot from the tail to the mouth without coming up."

Lola: "I can do it without the hookah."

Franco: "We may only get one chance. There's nothing to catch the hose this time. Arleen, feed the hose out to her from behind the floating transom."

Arleen: "I'm on it. I'll start it now."

Arleen gave the regulator to Lola to put in her mouth. She put the hair rope inside the back of the silver suit. She started the compressor. Lola took a breath and gave a thumbs up.

Lawanda: "What about me? This is my dream come true."

Franco: "Swim along the top from tail to mouth. I'll move off to the side and get you both. Remember, we are to observe but not touch or interfere with nature."

Franco went in first with his camera just behind the tail that waved slowly as the whale shark moved slowly forward. Lola slid in next to Franco, and Lawanda followed but stayed on the surface above the large, broad back. It was close enough that she could touch it. And she did.

Lola sank just below the tail and turned onto her back as she swam the underbelly. It was white and looked smooth. She didn't touch but wanted to. With her fins, she swam faster than the whale shark. Small schools of fish scattered as she moved forward and then back into place as she passed.

LOLA

Rich: "Incredible! You can see both of them top and bottom. Franco, you're a genius."

Lawanda: "Rough and hard. Not a fish skin."

Simone: "Hands off."

The whale shark coughed twice. Water burst from the front of her just as Lola reached the eye on one side of the head just past five gills on the side. Lawanda reached the other eye. Then they both swam around to the front.

Rich: "Look at the size of that mouth!"

Lawanda: "I can see the rows of small teeth around the opening. Rows and rows."

Gus was in the water ahead of the two women. He was ready. Then the whale shark opened its mouth.

Gus: "I could stand up in there."

The whale shark coughed again. The outflow pushed Lola and Lawanda back toward Gus. Mo had pulled the tender around so that he was in front of the group.

Arleen: "She wants help. She came to us for help."

Rich: "How do you know?"

Arleen: "I know."

Lola, Lawanda, and Gus floated in front of the giant with the giant mouth. They all looked inside at the hundreds of rows of small teeth, top, bottom, sides. Deep inside, they saw the throat where the food streamed in. To the sides were black sleeves, filters that caught debris before it could get into the throat or rows of gills. Stretched across the filters on the left-hand side was a section of net that had collected a sheet of plastic and various pieces of garbage.

Arleen: "Someone should go in there and take out that net."

Lawanda: "We're not to disturb nature."

Lola couldn't speak because of the hookah. She could see the problem. The whale shark sucked in water and pulled them closer but not inside. Lola could almost reach in and grab the net. The whale shark exhaled and pushed them away.

Lawanda: "I read about a woman who was sucked in by a whale shark. Then it spit her out without serious damage. I could go in and..."

Franco: "Not on your life. Look at those jaws."

Gus: "Looks like a size two to me."

Simone: "Lola, don't even think about it."

Lola had gotten close to the mouth again. She had thought about it. She knew the rules of research. She also knew her own heart.

Lawanda: "She's going to die if she can't breathe. She probably has pups inside."

Franco: "You have a pup inside. Our pup."

160

LOLA

Lola listened and faced the shark. She felt the hair rope Arleen had replaced in her silver suit.

She wondered what in the world was she doing here!

The decision was no longer hers. The whale shark opened its mouth and inhaled a large volume of water, and Lola was sucked in headfirst. Lola could still breathe through the hookah as she saw in the light from her mask camera the edge of the net. She grabbed it. The whale shark coughed and spit her out, followed by the net in her hand that she took with her. Another cough and garbage, plastic, paper, and dead fish were flushed from the filters.

Rich: "I can't believe this. Franco, did you get that?"

Franco: "Got it!"

Lola and Lawanda hugged when the whale shark put its head down and swam underneath them. She lifted her blunt nose to lift them and then dip them. She was playing with them.

Franco: "Lola, see if she'll take you for a ride."

Lawanda: "Do it, girl."

Lola drifted back to the top of the whale as it moved beneath her. She was careful not to touch the rough skin, but she caught the edge of the big dorsal fin. The whale shark waved its tail, and they swam along the wall.

Lola looked at the corals and fans that covered the wall. So many sea fans waving back and forth with the sea. The whale shark tail was waving back and forth with the same rhythm. The many-colored fish moved back and forth. Lola kicked her legs and moved her arms in the same way. Her body rolled from side to side. She was in tune with the sea. It all moved with the same rhythm. She felt the rapture. Lola was the sea.

The hookah mouthpiece suddenly jerked out of her mouth. She had reached the end of the line. She looked up.

Simone: "Eighty feet. Come up now!"

Lola looked up. The light at the surface was far away. She wasn't sure she could make it this time. She was doubtful. She was resigned to her fate. She had had a good life. It was the end.

"Never give up."

Lola reached for the light.

Gus was next to her in a heartbeat. The octopus rig he wore with his tank had an extra regulator. Lola took the mouthpiece and inhaled as she sat on Gus's hip, and they slowly went to the surface.
"Thank you, Gus," Lola said.
"It's my job, little sister," Gus said.

They came up next to the tender. Mo had on a mask. He was ready to go after them. He laughed when they came over the side into the tender.
"I was ready to pick you up," Mo said.
"It's a team sport." Gus blew him off. "That's why I make the big bucks."
"I'm glad I'm on your team," Lola said.

LOLA

Mo drove back to the floating transom where Lawanda was helping Franco with his equipment. He was a little slow. Lawanda eased him out flat on his back.

"You shouldn't have gone so deep," Lawanda said.

"I had to get the picture," Franco said. "The two of you with the shark from below silhouetted against the light from above. Once in a lifetime."

"Once in a dream come true," Lawanda said.

"Once," Lola said. "I don't want to do it again."

"Lola, come to the bridge," Simone called on the loudspeaker.

Arleen was standing with Rich as Simone ran the pictures from the mask cameras on the cockpit monitors. The center screen was the view from Lawanda as Lola was sucked into the mouth of the shark. Lawanda moved to grab Lola's fins before they disappeared inside. Then came the flood as Lola came out with the net in her hand. Then the garbage.

"Now we'll see what it looked like to Lola," Simone said.

The mouth was open to the incoming surge. A cloud of spawn and krill swirling about a hand that caught a rope. Then the flush out into Lawanda.

"That was amazing," Arleen said. "Were you scared?"

"I don't know," Lola said. "I was so focused on saving the whale shark that I didn't have time to think about me. I was on automatic. What happened happened. It was not as if I thought about choices. I was on a mission from the universe. I just went along for the ride."

"Mission accomplished," Rich said.

LOLA

"Thank God," Simone said. "We can look at the rest of these later. Right now, I have to get ready to perform a wedding before Rich leaves. Are Lawanda and Franco ready?"

"They were born ready," Arleen said.

Lola started to take off the silver suit, and the hair rope fell out of the back.

"Somebody always has your back," Arleen said.

Lola picked up the rope and waved it at Simone.

"There are so many things we can't explain," Simone said and winked at Arleen.

"Life is not always simple," Arleen said. "It's nothing to be concerned about."

"There are things in life worth being concerned about," Simone said. "This is not one of them. "

"I want to be out of here before sunset," Rich said. "The radar shows that hurricane has turned back this way."

"All hands on deck," came out over the loudspeaker.

Lola took a freshwater shower in Simone's room. Arleen came in with a pair of shorts and a sports bra. Lola couldn't find her brother's blue shirt.

"Lawanda says she can't fit into these things anymore," Arleen said. "I'm going to miss you."

"I can't find my rope sandals," Lola said.

"You'll have to go without them," Arleen said.

"I still have my hair rope," Lola said and tucked it into her hip pocket. "It's my only souvenir from my trip."

164

LOLA

The sun was in the western sky. Far to the east was a black line lit in places by distant lightning. There was not much of a breeze, and the seas were calm. The crew began to assemble on deck after the panels had been lowered.

Mo wore an Egyptian robe and prayer beads. Gus wore his short kaftan. Lawanda wore a white dress that Arleen had fashioned from a linen table cloth. Franco wore a collarless black shirt and black shorts. Rich wore a four-pocket shirt and cut-off jeans with a pair of well-worn leather boat shoes. Arleen wore Arleen.

Simone came down from the control room in her whites. She opened a manual that governed the powers of a ship's Captain. She read to herself before addressing the assembled crew. She closed the book and observed her flock. She smiled with satisfaction.

"I am so proud of what we were able to accomplish under such difficult conditions." Simone applauded. They applauded back. Simone wiped at her eyes but showed no tears.

"To our Captain," Gus said and brought out a bottle of rum that he sipped and then passed it to Rich, Lawanda, and Franco. Mo abstained, as did Arleen and Lola. When it got to Simone, she took a healthy pull and cleared her throat.

There were the distant flashes to the east behind where Simone stood. There was no thunder yet. The group took notice but were unmoved.

"We are gathered together," Simone began. "By the powers vested in me, I will unite this couple, Lawanda and Franco, in holy matrimony. Do you look forward with pleasure to seeing each other when you open your eyes in the morning or the middle of the night? Do you consider each other in making decisions without hesitation? Are you willing to spend eternity together beyond life and death?"

"We do," Lawanda and Franco said as one.

165

LOLA

"I now pronounce you man and wife," Simone said to cheers from the crowd.

There was a greater flash of light behind her. She turned toward it and touched her lips, kissed her fingertips, and placed them on the face of a man who stood next to her before he was gone in a second flash without thunder.

"Did you see him?" Arleen asked Lola.

"Yes," Lola said. "I'm sure I saw him."

They looked around at the others, who seemed more interested in the rum. Mo was on his knees in prayer. Franco and Lawanda were wrapped into one embrace that consumed the two of them.

"I hope that I can feel like that someday," Lola said.

Mo had gotten up and was next to her. She looked at the tall, dark man who inspected her from top to bottom. She was uncomfortable.

"I will marry you in a couple of years," Mo said. "If you still are a virgin."

"Two years is a long time," Lola said.

"Three years is longer," Arleen said and moved them away.

"I could make you into the world's best free diver," Mo called after them. "You are a natural."

Gus was next to them with the rum that he continued to sip. He didn't bother to offer it to the girls. He couldn't stand rejection.

"You could have made it without me," Gus told Lola. "I just made it easier. You didn't think you were going to die?"

"No," Lola said. "I thought I was going to fail."

LOLA

"You finished," Gus said. "That's what counts. Now you're done, and we have no use for you. The Silver Bullet is wrapped. You can go back to being who you are."

"Who are you?" Arleen said.

"I'm a daughter. I'm a sister. I'm a swimmer, and I probably have to study for the Finals," Lola said. "This was all just a break in the routine."

"You are who you are," Arleen said. "Titles diminish you. "

"I'm going to miss you," Gus said. "You brought vitality to this project. For the next project, we will do some underwater shots for a new James Bond movie. He's not a size two. We're going to have to find somebody to replace Rich too. For the deck crew."

"I have someone in mind," Arleen said.

Franco and Lawanda joined them and took over the bottle. They shared a couple of sips. Lawanda refused, rubbing her belly. They embraced Lola in a threesome.

"Thank you for being my alter ego," Lawanda said with a wet kiss on Lola's cheek.

"You saved the day," Franco said.

"But my name will still appear in the credits," Lawanda said.

"I'll send you the outtakes," Franco said. "The rest belongs to *National Geographic*."

"You can't even see my face," Lola said.

"An uncredited co-contributor," Franco said.

"An unindicted co-conspirator," Gus said.

"That's show biz," Arleen said.

"You're not even on the payroll." Rich moved them aside. "My helicopter is about to arrive."

LOLA

"Clear the deck," Simone shouted as the beat of the copter blades became louder, and the sky darkened with the first drops of rain. Everyone hurried to their rooms. "We need to get you out of here in a hurry."

"We saw Philippe," Lola told her.
"Of course you did," Simone said. "There are more things than Heaven and Earth."

The helicopter dropped down from the sky ahead of the storm. It made its own wind and roar. It settled amidships with plenty of room clear of the control tower and bridge. It was big. Not as big as the whale shark, but it was impressive.

Lola had never been on a helicopter. There were new experiences every day. She was in a hurry to board behind Rich, who carried a laptop computer, a Dopp bag for toiletries, and a small sack for his clothes that he wasn't wearing. A door on the side of the copter slid back, and three metal steps dropped down. The inside was brightly lit now that the sun was fading. Lola only carried her cellphone and what she wore. She was barefoot as she climbed the steps that reminded her of the ladder on the cruise ship that seemed so long ago.

Inside the helicopter was a large cabin with six tan leather reclining seats. The flight deck was in front of the cabin where two pilots flew the airship. Outside, the crew of the *Bob Marley* assembled in the rain as the door slid shut.

"Lola, Lola, Lola, Lola, Lola..." They all shouted and pumped their fists in the air.

LOLA

The door slid shut and blocked out the chants and the rotor noise.

"White sound insulation," Rich said. "It blocks out the extraneous clutter. I have a company that developed it."

He buckled himself into a seat behind Lola. He was already into his computer as he put on a headset to communicate with the pilots. He said something, and up they went.

Lola was happy to be going home. She also felt a sadness as she left her crewmates behind. She looked down at Gus, Mo, Lawanda, Franco, and Arleen.

Arleen was wearing her blue shirt and rope sandals. She waved wildly and laughed loud enough to be heard above the white noise. The others began busying themselves as Simone headed the ship west. The helicopter also flew toward the sun.

Above the clouds, the sun still shined. A layer of puffy rolling clouds lay below. A skyscape of white boulders hung above. Mountainous formations were a panorama in the distance. Pillars of twisting white plumes stood between the layers. Fountains of white spouted up in undetermined places. Then they were above it all into the other big blue.

The sky.

Lola was mesmerized by the variety of forms as she had been when viewing the life on the reefs. As they veered to the north, around the storm, a towering cloud had anviled out at the top. They rose above its gray shelf. The ride became bumpy. Lola rode with the wind. She had been the sea. Now she was the sky.

"This is the last of that hurricane," Rich said over her shoulder. "The storm has passed. The *Bob Marley* can now go into dry dock and replace that patch you made."

169

LOLA

Not in the credits. Not on the payroll. No pictures of her face. And no patch that she put in place. Lola thought it was like she had never been there.

The sun was at the top of the mountainous clouds but sank into a red, orange, and gold horizon. The yellow balloon sank into the clouds and down into the sea. Soon it was night.

Lola felt an inner longing. She missed her crewmates. She also missed her family and her own bed with its stuffed animals and down pillows. There was no place like home Toto. But something was lacking. Where was the sense of adventure? Where was the struggle and triumph? Finals were boring compared to the mouth of a whale shark.

The wind took the helicopter to new heights. Lola's ears popped. Her hands gripped the arms of the seat. Her heart raced. She breathed her breaths and centered herself for whatever fate had in store. Would she be rescued at sea?

"The air is just like the sea," Rich comforted her. "It is the sea in a vaporous form. We are living in gas rather than in liquid. It's all the sea. We are all the sea."

Lola was too tired to contemplate deep thoughts. The day had begun with an enchanted swim and ended in the mouth of a whale shark. It is my life. She had been from the bottom of the sea to the top of the clouds. The stars were coming out, and she was drifting in endless space. The space was sleep.

LOLA

There was a small private airport not far from Lola's house. As they landed, she could see her mother, father, and brother waiting. She took off her seatbelt before the door slid open.

"You have been the highlight of my vacation," Rich said. "I'll be in touch. Tell your folks I said hello, but I don't have time to stop. Business, you know. I have a lot of money to spend. You have something more valuable than my money. You have my friendship."

The door slid shut behind Lola, and the helicopter lifted, blowing her into the arms of her family. They were full of hugs, tears, and kisses. And questions.

"Where have you been?" Lola's mother asked. "We've been worried sick."

They got into the car parked by the runway. Her brother drove with her father upfront. Lola sat with her mother in the back.

"I told you she would be alright," her brother said. She could see his smile in the rearview mirror.

"I talked to my intelligence friend in Miami," her father said. "That picture on the *Malecon* wasn't you. It was an actress named Lola Lobo who was making a movie in Cuba. She looked a lot like you."

Lola felt for the hair rope in her back pocket. It was still there. She rested against her mother, inhaling a scent of lavender and emotion.

"You can stay home tomorrow if you like," her mother said. "But you do have swim practice, a math test, and Finals. You decide."

Lola was too tired to speak. It was wonderful to be in a familiar place with people who knew who she really was.

Really?

LOLA

The lights in the house were all on. There was a "Welcome Home" sign above the dining room table. There was her favorite chocolate cake.

"Rich called us last night," her father said. "He told us when you would be here. Welcome home, Lola."

"I missed you," her brother said.

Lola stuck her finger in the icing on the cake and licked it.

"Where are your manners?" her mother said. "Who have you been hanging out with?"

"Later," Lola said. "Right now, I just want to crawl into my bed and breathe."

"Give me those salty-looking clothes," her mother said. "I'll put them in the wash."

Lola took the hair rope from her pocket and put it on the night stand next to her bed with her cellphone. She took off her clothes and put them outside the bedroom door. She got in bed with her favorite stuffed animal, a velvet dolphin. She was naked. She could leave the *Bob Marley*, but the *Bob Marley* wouldn't leave her.

Goodnight, Arleen.

Lola was fast asleep. She was dreaming about her journey when she saw a man at the foot of her bed. The lights were off, but she could see he was wet and raw. It was Manuel.

"*Langostina*," he said. "You have something I need."

"I owe you so much," Lola said. "Anything I have is yours, but not my dolphin."

Lola hugged her stuffed animal. She pulled the sheets over her head. She went back to sleep.

LOLA

"You were talking in your sleep last night," Lola's mother said. "You look a little pale. You haven't gotten enough sun lately. Maybe you should take a day off."

Pale? Maybe it's from being in that silver suit all day, Lola thought. She tried to rub the sleep from her eyes. What a strange dream!

Maybe it was all a dream. She was just an ordinary girl with hopes and dreams. She was not a hero.

What was flows into what will be. That's what is. She needed proof of her journey. Her clothes were gone. There was no hair rope on the nightstand with her cellphone. She was not in the film's credits. She was not on the payroll. Her face wasn't in any of the recordings. There was no proof. It was all a dream that she had been a hero for a while. But it was all a dream.

Lola's cellphone rang.

Victor. " Beautiful woman, I can't get you out of my mind."

There was his face on the statue of "The Thinker."

Lola: "I look forward to seeing you again."

Another message: Familia Cubana: "Lola my sister I miss you. We have internet today." Juanita.
Lola:" Patria y vida. BFF."

Lola's brother yelled from the other room.
"Arleen called me," he said. "She said I can take Rich's place in the crew for the next project. If he can run a billion-dollar empire, I can run my small startup. She said she'll teach me to dive."

173

LOLA

"You know how to dive," Lola said.

His smile showed through the wall.

"What do you think I'll need?" he asked.

"If you need anything, Arleen will get it for you." Lola returned the smile.

"Better get up," her mother called. "Some people are calling from the State Department who want to talk to you. They say they just want to ask you a few questions."

Lola slid out of the bottom of her bed. She was standing in the water. Seawater. It looked like two wet footprints where Manuel had stood in her dream. He needed the hair rope to regain his identity. Manuel the long-haired...

"The dream was not a dream," Lola said.

"I am a hero."

THE END

LOLA

Other works by the author

A GIFT FOR A LIFETIME Anthology (Amazon)
A DAY AT THE BEACH Novella (Amazon)
MURDER IN KEY WEST Novel (Amazon)
THE GIRL IN THE BLACK BOOTS Novel (Amazon)
MONEY BAY Screenplay (Amazon)
Ernest Hemingway's
THE FIFTH COLUMN
Screen treatment (Amazon)
CREDIT-LIFE
Stageplay
COFFEE AT STARBUCKS
One act play